Chasing Dreams

ANNIE SEATON

Duckinwilla Days: Book 4

Heartwarming and compelling tales of love, self-discovery, and second chances in the heart of rural Australia.

The Johnson family

Grandmère and Papa: Margot and Robert Johnson

The parents: Hugo and Ellen Johnson

The Johnson siblings:

Charlotte Johnson - Book 1 - *Coming Home*

Julien Johnson -Book 2 - *Secrets and Surprises*

Oliver Johnson - Book 3 – *Wishes and Whispers*

Guy Johnson - Book 4 – *Chasing Dreams*

Amelia Johnson - Book 5 – *New Beginnings*

Lisette Johnson - Book 6 - *Together at Last*

CHASING DREAMS

Chapter 1

The pre-dawn air carried a crisp edge that spoke of autumn's approach, though the Queensland heat would return with vengeance once the sun climbed higher. Guy Johnson stood at the kitchen window, coffee mug warming his hands as he watched the eastern paddocks emerge from shadow. The cane was looking good this season—tall and healthy, swaying gently in the morning breeze that drifted in from the coast. Arrows were beginning to form at the tops of the stalks in a couple of the smaller paddocks as the weather cooled.

Three months had passed since the family's return from France, and life had settled back into its familiar rhythm. Almost. The farmhouse seemed happier, with Oliver's contentment casting a warm glow over everything. His brother's relationship with Sarah had transformed Oliver—and as Mum and Charlotte planned the upcoming wedding, significant glances were thrown in his and Sarah's direction when the family were together.

'You're up early,' Amelia's voice interrupted his thoughts as she padded into the kitchen, hair tousled and currently a subdued shade of burgundy. She'd toned down the more dramatic colours since Myron had left for Brisbane, though Guy suspected that had more to do with her general mood than making a statement.

'Couldn't sleep,' he replied, taking another sip of his coffee. 'I want to check the irrigation timers before the ag college students arrive.'

Amelia poured herself a mug from the pot he'd made, adding enough sugar to make his teeth ache just watching. 'What ag students?'

'Elena's coming back today, and we've got two students from Gatton interested in looking at our water management as part of a study the college is doing.' Guy tried to keep his tone casual, but something must have shown in his expression because Amelia's eyebrows rose with interest.

'Elena? The Brazilian girl who was here before Christmas?'

'That's the one.' Guy rinsed his mug in the

sink, avoiding his sister's knowing eyes. 'She knows a lot about sustainable farming practices we could implement.'

'Uh-huh.' Amelia settled onto a kitchen stool, clearly in no hurry to let the subject drop. 'And it has nothing to do with the fact that you spent half the harvest season discussing water conservation techniques with her?'

Guy shot her a warning look. 'It's about the farm, Amelia. Dad's interested in diversifying our methods, and Elena's worked on operations twice our size in Brazil.'

'Of course it is.' Amelia's grin was positively feline. 'Just like Oliver's sudden interest in the Bargara markets was purely about expanding our customer base.' She looked around, and he was pleased when she changed the subject. 'Where's Mum and Dad?'

'They've gone to Brisbane, remember?'

'Dad okay?'

Before Guy could reply, the sound of tyres on gravel announced the new arrivals. Through the window, he spotted Elena's beat-up blue sedan pulling up beside the equipment shed.

'Showtime,' Amelia murmured, but when

Guy glanced at her, her expression was bland. 'For what it's worth, Guy, I liked her. She's got that same quiet intensity as you. Very... compatible.'

Guy felt heat creep up his neck. 'She's a worker, Amelia, and leaving in three months. Going back to Brazil to run her family's farm.'

'A lot can happen in three months,' his sister replied with a shrug. 'Look at Oliver and Sarah. And Charlotte and Greg.'

That was different, Guy wanted to say, but he held back. What he and Elena had was hard to describe. Professional respect, certainly. A connection that went deeper than farming techniques, if he was honest. But she'd been clear from the beginning that Australia was just one stop on her journey, not a destination, so he'd tried to keep his distance. Most of the time.

The screen door banged behind Guy as the arrivals made their way towards the house, Elena's familiar silhouette moving with the confident stride he remembered. She wore practical work clothes—faded jeans, a long-sleeved shirt rolled to her elbows, sturdy boots that had seen plenty of use. Her dark hair was pulled back in a braid that hung between her shoulder blades, and even from a distance, Guy could see the easy smile she offered the others.

'I'll go show them around,' he called through the door.

'Guy,' Amelia yelled out.

When he came back to the door, her expression was uncharacteristically serious. 'Don't let the fact that something might be temporary stop you from seeing what it could become.'

Before he could reply, she'd disappeared upstairs, leaving him to face the day—and Elena—with Amelia's cryptic advice echoing in his mind.

***

Elena Santiago had forgotten how quiet mornings at the Johnson farm could be. In São Paulo, where she'd spent the last two months consulting with agricultural researchers, the city woke with a cacophony of traffic and construction. But here at Duckinwilla Creek, the only sounds were the distant lowing of cattle and the soft rustle of leaves in the breeze.

She'd also forgotten how the light was here, softer somehow, the low autumn mist making the farm sheds look like something from a painting. Or maybe she was just seeing it through different eyes now, knowing this would be her final stop before heading home again. This time for good.

The two students she'd met in the Lockyer Valley—Ben and Marcus, both in their twenties and eager to prove themselves—had chatted nonstop during the drive from town, where she had picked them up off the bus. Elena had let their conversation wash over her, content to reacquaint herself with the landscape that had captured her imagination during the harvest season's brief stint with the Johnsons.

Now, as Guy emerged from the farmhouse, she felt that familiar flutter of... what? Anticipation? Nervousness? It was hard to define the effect he had on her, this quiet man who was more interested in sustainable farming than anyone she'd met in her three years of agricultural travel.

'Elena,' he said as she approached, his voice carrying that same warmth she remembered. 'Good to have you back.' He held out his hand,

and as she took it, the zing that ran up her arm unsettled her.

'Good to be back,' she replied, and meant it. Of all the farms she'd worked on, all the operations she'd studied, something about this place had resonated with her. The Johnsons ran their farm with a combination of traditional knowledge and innovative thinking that reminded her of home, of the challenges her own family faced with their coffee plantation in Brazil.

She introduced Guy to Ben and Marcus, then he launched into the routine tour that Elena remembered from her first visit. But this time, she found herself paying attention to different details—the way Guy's hands moved when he explained the irrigation system, the quiet pride in his voice when he described their sustainable practices, the ease with which he handled the younger workers' questions.

'Elena worked with us last harvest,' Guy said as they paused beside the eastern paddock. 'She's got experience with water conservation techniques that we're hoping to incorporate this year.'

Ben, a lanky redhead with calloused hands that spoke of previous farm work, looked impressed. 'You're from Brazil, right? I heard the farms there are massive.'

'Some are,' Elena confirmed. 'My family's operation is smaller—more like this one. Coffee as well as cane, but similar challenges.'

'Elena's going back to implement some new systems after harvest,' Guy added. 'She's been studying operations like ours across Australia for the past three years.'

'And I've learned a lot,' she said with a wide smile at Guy. His eyes held hers, and she made herself look away. While Guy was a very good-looking guy, she didn't need another complication in her life.

The tour continued through the machinery shed, to the greenhouse where Oliver had been experimenting with heritage mango varieties, and finally to the newly renovated quarters where the students would be staying. Elena would be in the same small cabin she'd occupied before—basic but comfortable, with a view across the paddocks towards the creek.

'Lunch is at noon in the house,' Guy

explained as they finished the tour. 'Elena knows the routine, but we'll all eat together for the first week while everyone settles in. After that, you're welcome to join us or make your own arrangements.'

As Ben and Marcus headed off to settle into their quarters, Elena lingered beside Guy in the shade of the machinery shed. The heat was building now, and she could hear the distant hum of irrigation systems starting their daily cycle.

'How was your visit home?' Guy asked, his tone casual.

'Productive,' Elena replied, then found herself elaborating. 'The university in São Paulo has been developing some interesting approaches to drought-resistant crops. Not directly applicable to cane, but the principles are sound.'

'And the research facility in Queensland?'

Elena smiled, remembering their email correspondence while she'd been away. Guy had been unfailingly polite in his messages, sharing updates about the farm's progress and asking thoughtful questions about her research. But there had been something beneath the professional courtesy—a warmth that had made her look forward to each message more than she usually did.

'The Queensland facility was fascinating,' she said. 'They're doing incredible work with soil microbiomes. Some of their techniques could transform how we approach organic certification in Brazil. One of the professors suggested Ben and Marcus could be useful to my… our work here.'

Guy nodded, his interest genuine. This was what she appreciated about him—his ability to understand not just the technical aspects of farming, but the broader implications for communities and families who depended on the land.

'I've been thinking about your water collection system,' he said, gesturing towards the paddocks. 'The one you mentioned last season. We had good rains over the winter, but if this drought pattern continues...'

'I've brought some updated diagrams with me,' Elena interrupted, surprising herself with her eagerness. 'Based on what I learned in São Paulo, some of the modifications could increase your efficiency by twenty percent.'

Guy's smile was wide. 'I'd like to see those. Tonight, maybe? After dinner?'

Elena nodded, pleased that Guy was still keen. 'Of course. I'll bring them to the main house after the others have settled in.'

'How about we meet in the living area of the quarters? It'll be quieter than our place now that everyone's home.'

'Yes, I am happy with that.'

A horn honked from the direction of the farmhouse; the sound broke their comfortable silence, and Guy took a step back.

'I should let you get settled,' he said, his no-nonsense tone returning. 'I'll see you about seven-thirty?'

Elena nodded, watching as he headed towards the house with that efficient stride she remembered. Only when he'd disappeared around the corner did she allow herself to acknowledge the truth she'd been avoiding since she'd asked to return to the Johnson farm.

She'd come back for the farming techniques and the sustainable practices, yes. But she'd also come back to see more of Guy—the quiet man who listened more than he spoke and whose rare smiles could light up his entire face. The man who would still be here, long after she'd returned to Brazil and the responsibilities waiting for her there.

It was going to be an interesting three months.

***

Guy found Oliver in the kitchen, unpacking crates of mangoes with the focused attention he usually reserved for selecting seed varieties. His brother looked up as Guy entered, a grin spreading across his face.

'Good morning at the markets,' Oliver said by way of greeting. 'Sarah's soap display drew quite a crowd. We're thinking about setting up a permanent weekend stall here on the farm.'

'That's great,' Guy replied, though his attention was distracted. Through the window, he could see Elena helping the two new workers carry their gear to the quarters.

Oliver followed his gaze, then set down the mango he'd been examining. 'Elena's back.'

It wasn't a question, and Guy didn't bother

pretending he hadn't been watching her. 'Started this morning. She'll be here until mid-harvest.'

'And then?'

'Then she goes back to Brazil. Her family's farm.' Guy opened the refrigerator, more for something to do with his hands than because he needed anything.

Oliver leaned against the counter. 'Don't get too used to her being here.'

Guy shot him a look. 'What's that supposed to mean?'

'You've talked about her a lot since she was here.' Oliver selected another mango, testing its ripeness as he stared intently at Guy. 'You've been checking your email more often since she left. And unless my memory's failing, you spent most of last season finding excuses to work wherever she was working.'

Heat crept up Guy's neck. 'She's knowledgeable about sustainable farming. It makes sense to—'

'Guy.' Oliver's voice was gentle but firm. 'I'm not hassling you. I'm just saying maybe don't write off something before you've given it a real chance.'

Before Guy could respond, Amelia burst through the kitchen door with her usual theatrical flair, her burgundy hair catching the light as she moved.

'I'm so pleased Elena's back!' she announced, as if this were breaking news. 'I saw her helping those new boys with their gear. Such a gentleman, our Elena.'

'Gentlewoman,' Oliver corrected with a smirk.

'You know what I mean.' Amelia waved a dismissive hand. 'She's got that whole capable, competent thing going on. Very attractive in a woman, don't you think, Guy?'

Guy felt like he was being tag-teamed by his siblings. 'I think she's here to work, and so are the rest of us.'

'Of course she is,' Amelia agreed readily. 'But that doesn't mean—'

'Don't start,' Guy warned, recognising the gleam in his sister's eyes. 'Whatever matchmaking scheme you're cooking up, don't. Elena's not Sarah. She's not looking to settle down in rural Queensland.'

Amelia exchanged a look with Oliver that

Guy didn't like at all.

'Who said anything about settling down?' she asked innocently. 'I just think it's nice to have competent help around the farm. Someone who appreciates good, sustainable farming practices.'

'And speaks Portuguese,' Oliver added unhelpfully. 'Didn't you say you've been learning Portuguese, Guy?'

Guy stared at his brother. 'How the hell did you—'

'Language app notifications on your phone,' Oliver said with a grin. 'You left it on the kitchen counter last week. Duolingo's very persistent about daily practice.'

'I was just—' Guy began, then stopped. There was no point denying it. He *had* been learning Portuguese, telling himself it was just a way to better understand the farming techniques Elena described. But if he was honest, it had more to do with wanting to understand her world, the place she came from. The place she'd be returning to in three months.

'Just what?' Amelia prompted, her grin matching Oliver's.

'Just trying to improve my language skills,' Guy finished lamely.

'Of course you were,' Amelia said, patting his arm with mock sympathy. 'Very sensible. Never know when Portuguese might come in handy on a Queensland cane farm.'

The sound of voices outside saved Guy from further teasing. Elena was approaching the house with Ben and Marcus. He smoothed down his shirt, then immediately felt foolish for the gesture.

'Lunch is ready,' he announced, moving towards the stove where a pot of Amelia's vegetable soup was warming. 'Nothing fancy, but—'

'It smells wonderful,' Elena said as she entered the kitchen, and Guy felt that familiar warmth of awareness at the sound of her voice. She'd changed from her work clothes into a simple blue shirt and clean jeans, and somehow managed to make even that basic outfit look effortlessly elegant.

'Elena!' Amelia immediately swept her into a hug that Elena returned with evident pleasure. 'How was São Paulo? And that research facility near Brisbane? Guy mentioned you'd been there.'

'Both very productive,' Elena replied, accepting the bowl of soup Guy offered her. 'I've learned some techniques that could be useful here, if you're interested.'

'Always interested in new ideas,' Oliver said, settling at the kitchen table. 'That's how we keep improving. We just have to convince Dad that change is not necessarily a bad thing.'

As they ate, the conversation flowed easily between farming techniques, Elena's research experiences, and updates on the family's French adventure.

'So, what's the plan for tomorrow?' Ben asked as they finished eating. 'Guy mentioned starting with the eastern paddock.'

'Routine maintenance first,' Guy explained. 'Checking irrigation lines, testing soil moisture levels, that sort of thing. Elena, I thought you might want to see how the modifications we discussed last season worked out.'

Elena's eyes lit up with professional interest. 'The drainage improvements? How did they perform during the summer?'

'Better than expected,' Guy replied, pleased to see her enthusiasm. 'We had some significant rainfall in January, and the new channels handled it without any flooding issues.'

'That's excellent.'

As lunch wound down and everyone dispersed to their afternoon tasks, Guy lingered in the kitchen with a cup of tea as Amelia stacked the dishwasher.

'Well, I've got work to do,' he announced as he passed her his mug. 'I'll head out to the shed.'

'Don't we all,' Amelia replied cheerfully. 'Oh look, there goes Elena to the shed now. You'd better hurry, or you'll miss her.'

Guy escaped before she could say anything else, but Amelia's chuckle followed him out. As he walked towards the shed, he tried to convince himself that meeting Elena tonight really was just about farming techniques and water management systems.

He was a terrible liar, even to himself.

Chapter 2

The communal room of the workers' accommodation had taken on a different quality by seven-thirty. The harsh afternoon light had softened to the soft glow of dusk streaming through the wide windows, and the day's work had been done. The large space, with its mismatched furniture and communal kitchen area, felt more intimate in the evening light.

Guy had showered and changed into clean clothes—a decision he'd questioned three times before settling on dark jeans and a collared shirt. He'd claimed one of the round tables near the kitchen area, away from the television, where Ben was watching the evening news.

Elena arrived precisely on time, carrying a leather portfolio that looked well-travelled and a laptop that had seen better days. She'd changed too, into a flowing skirt and fitted top that made Guy momentarily forget why she was there. Ben glanced up as she entered, offering a polite nod before returning to the news.

'Coffee?' Guy offered, gesturing towards

the pot he'd prepared using the communal facilities. 'Or would you prefer tea?'

'Coffee would be good, thank you,' Elena replied, settling into the plastic chair across from him and opening her portfolio. 'I've been thinking about your drainage system since lunch. The modifications you made were clever, but I think we can improve on them.'

Guy poured two cups of coffee from the shared pot, adding milk to his own and leaving Elena's black, the way he remembered she preferred it.

'Show me what you've got,' he said, settling back into his chair.

Elena spread several hand-drawn diagrams across the scratched table surface, weighted down at the corners with salt and pepper shakers. Her drawings were precise and detailed, annotated in a mixture of English and Portuguese that Guy found himself trying to decipher. Around them, the gentle hum of the television and the distant sound of Marcus washing their dinner dishes in the communal sink created a backdrop of noise.

'The basic principle is gravity-fed

distribution,' Elena explained, her finger tracing the lines on the diagram. 'But instead of relying purely on slope, we incorporate a series of collection basins that can redirect flow based on soil saturation levels.'

Guy leaned forward, studying the intricate network of channels and basins she'd mapped out. 'This would require significant earthworks,' he observed. 'How do you manage that without disrupting existing crop lines?'

'Ah, that's the beauty of it,' Elena said, her enthusiasm evident in the way her eyes lit up. 'You phase the installation over multiple seasons. Start with the collection points during fallow periods, then connect them gradually as you rotate the cane planting.'

She pulled out another diagram, this one showing a timeline that stretched across three planting cycles. Guy found himself impressed not just by the technical innovation but by the careful planning that would make implementation practical for a working farm.

'In Brazil, my family's farm implemented something similar over five years,' Elena continued. 'The initial investment was significant, but our water efficiency improved by thirty percent, and we eliminated erosion issues that had been problematic for decades.'

'Thirty percent,' Guy repeated, calculating the implications. 'That kind of improvement could transform our entire operation.'

'Exactly. And with the climate patterns you've been experiencing here—extended dry periods followed by intense rainfall—this kind of system becomes essential for long-term sustainability.'

They bent over the diagrams together for over an hour, discussing technical details and potential modifications for Queensland conditions. Guy found himself increasingly absorbed in Elena's explanations, impressed by the depth of her knowledge and the practical experience that informed her suggestions. At one point, he was vaguely aware of Ben and Marcus saying goodnight.

'This collection basin here,' he said, pointing to a junction in her design. 'How do you prevent sediment buildup without regular maintenance?'

Elena smiled, leaning closer to show him the

detail he'd missed. 'Self-cleaning design. The flow pattern creates a scouring action that carries sediment through to the main drainage channel.'

Her proximity made it difficult for Guy to concentrate on the technical aspects of her explanation. She smelled faintly of lime and something indefinably tropical, and when she moved to point out another feature, her shoulder brushed against his.

'Guy?' Elena's voice brought him back to the present. 'Did you have a question about the overflow mechanism?'

'Sorry,' he said, feeling heat rise in his cheeks. 'I was thinking about implementation logistics.'

'Of course.' Elena's tone was perfectly professional, but Guy caught something in her expression—a flicker of awareness that suggested she was aware of their proximity too.

They worked through the diagrams systematically, discussing costs, timelines, and potential challenges. Elena's laptop provided additional details and photos from similar installations, including several from her family's farm that gave Guy his first real glimpse into her world.

'Your coffee plantation is beautiful,' he said, studying a photo of terraced slopes covered in glossy-leafed bushes. 'How long has it been in your family?'

'Five generations,' Elena replied, her voice carrying a note of pride. 'My great-great-grandfather started with twenty hectares. Now we have over two hundred.'

'And you'll be taking over when you return?'

Elena frowned. 'Taking over, expanding, modernising—it's a significant responsibility. My father's been managing things while I've been travelling, but he's eager to retire. My brothers...' She shrugged, and a whiff of lime came his way. 'They have other interests.'

Guy sensed her hesitation; it was something he understood. His family expected that he would take over, too.

'That's a lot of pressure,' he said quietly.

'It is,' Elena agreed. 'But also an incredible opportunity. The techniques I've learned here, in Australia, they could transform our operation. Make it more sustainable, more productive, better for the environment and the community.'

'You sound excited about it,' Guy observed, though he thought he detected a note of uncertainty beneath her enthusiasm.

'I am excited. Most of the time.' Elena closed her laptop and began gathering the diagrams. 'It's just... big. The changes I want to make, the investments required—there's a lot of risk involved.'

'Change always involves risk,' Guy said. 'But from what I've seen of your work, your family's lucky to have you.'

Elena looked up from her papers, meeting his gaze directly. 'Thank you. That means a lot, coming from you.'

Her words hung between them as Guy studied her face; the determined line of her jaw, the intelligence in her dark eyes, the way her hair had escaped its braid to frame her face in soft tendrils.

'I should let you get some rest,' Elena said, standing and gathering her materials. 'Tomorrow will be a long day.'

'Elena,' Guy said as she reached the door. When she turned back, he found himself at a loss for words. What could he say? That he'd enjoyed their evening together more than any business meeting had a right to be enjoyed? That he was looking forward to tomorrow's work because it meant more time with her? 'Thank you for sharing your ideas,' he settled on finally. 'I think we can make something special happen here.'

Elena smiled, and Guy's heart skipped. 'I think so too. Goodnight, Guy.'

'Goodnight.'

Guy remained in the kitchen long after Elena had gone, staring at the table where her diagrams had been spread. The lingering scent of her perfume mixed with the aroma of cooling coffee, and he could still see her animated expressions as she'd explained her ideas.

Three months, he reminded himself. She would be here for three months, and then she would return to Brazil and the responsibilities waiting for her there. He wouldn't see her again. Whatever this growing attraction was, it had a built-in expiration date.

The sensible thing would be to keep their relationship professional, to appreciate her expertise without letting it become personal. Guy had always been the sensible brother—the one who planned carefully, thought things through, and avoided unnecessary complications.

But as he cleaned up the coffee cups and turned off the kitchen lights, Guy couldn't shake the feeling that Elena Santiago might be the most beautiful complication his life had ever encountered.

***

Elena's cabin was dark and quiet, but sleep eluded her. She lay on the narrow bed, staring at the ceiling and listening to the night sounds of the Australian countryside—the distant lowing of cattle, the rustle of small creatures in the grass, the whisper of wind through the cane fields.

Her laptop was open on the small desk by the window, displaying an email from her father that had arrived while she'd been with Guy. The message was brief and to the point, as always: the farm was doing well, but he was looking forward to her return and the implementation of the improvements she'd been researching.

The new processing equipment arrived last week, he'd written. *I've had it installed in the main facility, but I haven't attempted to operate it yet. That will be your project when you come home.*

Home. The word should have filled Elena with anticipation, with excitement about the changes she could make and the legacy she would inherit. Instead, she found herself thinking about Guy's quiet intensity as he'd studied her diagrams, the way his eyes had lit up when he understood the implications of her innovations.

She turned onto her side, looking out the window towards the main house. Most of the lights were off now, but she could see a warm glow from what she thought might be the kitchen window. Was Guy still up, perhaps thinking about their conversation as she was?

Elena sat up abruptly, annoyed with herself. This was exactly the kind of thinking that would lead to complications she couldn't afford. She was here for three months to complete her research and gain practical experience with Australian farming techniques. Getting emotionally involved with Guy Johnson wasn't part of the plan.

But as she settled back onto the pillow, Elena couldn't deny the growing attraction she felt for the quiet man whose rare smile had the power to make her forget all her carefully laid plans.

Three months suddenly seemed both impossibly long and far too short.

Chapter 3

At dawn, mist rose from the irrigation channels in the eastern paddock, creating veils that drifted between the rows of young cane. The air was cool and sweet, carrying the earthy scent of rich soil and the sweetness of sugar. Guy stood at the edge of the field, coffee mug in hand, as the rising sun painted the sky in shades of rose and gold.

He'd been awake since four-thirty, unable to shake the restless energy that had plagued him since last night's meeting. Elena's diagrams were still spread across his desk, annotated with additional notes he'd made when he went back to the house. The more he studied her proposals, the more convinced he became that they represented exactly the kind of innovation the farm needed.

The sound of footsteps on gravel announced Elena's arrival. She appeared through the morning mist like a character from a movie scene, her hair braided back and secured with a blue bandana, work clothes practical but somehow elegant on her muscular frame.

'Morning,' she called, her voice carrying easily in the still air. 'Beautiful sunrise.'

'It is,' Guy agreed, though he found himself looking at her rather than the sky. 'Sleep well?'

'Well enough,' Elena replied. 'I was thinking about your soil composition. The drainage modifications I showed you last night will work better if we understand the subsurface clay distribution.'

Guy nodded, relieved to have concrete work to focus on. 'I've got soil samples from three months ago, but we should probably take fresh ones from the areas where you're proposing the collection basins.'

They set off into the paddock, following the irrigation channels that Guy had installed two seasons ago. The system was functional but basic—a network of concrete channels that carried water from the main line to the crop rows. Elena walked the perimeter thoughtfully; occasionally stopping to examine the flow patterns or test the soil with a small auger she'd produced from her bag.

'The existing infrastructure is solid,' she observed, crouching beside one of the main distribution points. 'But you're losing a lot of efficiency through evaporation and runoff.'

'I know,' Guy admitted. 'Dad's been resistant to major modifications. He prefers incremental improvements over system overhauls.'

Elena glanced up at him. 'But you don't?'

'I think sometimes you have to take bigger risks to achieve meaningful change,' Guy said, then heat rose in his cheeks as he realised how his words could be taken.

If Elena noticed his discomfort, she didn't comment on it. Instead, she stood and moved to the next sampling point, her movements practical.

'In Brazil,' she said as they worked, 'my father was the same way initially. Gradual changes, traditional methods, minimal risk. It took three years of crop failures before he was willing to consider radical modifications.'

'What changed his mind?'

Elena's expression grew serious. 'Necessity. The climate patterns shifted, and our traditional approaches weren't sustainable anymore. We had to adapt or lose the farm.'

'That must have been difficult.'

'Terrifying,' Elena corrected. 'But also liberating in a way. When you're forced to innovate, you discover capabilities you didn't know you had.'

They worked for an hour, taking soil samples and discussing potential modifications to the existing system. Elena's expertise was evident in every suggestion she made, but Guy found himself equally impressed by her ability to understand the broader context—the family dynamics, the financial constraints, the delicate balance between innovation and preservation that defined generational farming.

'Guy!' Oliver's voice called from the direction of the farmhouse. 'Amelia's cooked breakfast. She said to hurry up because she has to leave soon.'

Elena straightened, wiping soil from her hands with a clean cloth. 'Shall we continue this after we eat?'

'Definitely,' Guy replied, gathering the soil samples they'd collected. 'I want to hear more about your phased implementation approach.'

As they walked back towards the house, Elena fell into step beside him, her stride matching his easily. 'You know,' she said, 'I've worked on a lot of farms during my travels. Most of them view sustainability as a burden—something they have to do to meet regulations or satisfy consumers. But you approach it differently.'

'How so?'

'You see it as an opportunity. A way to improve not just your operation, but your relationship with the land itself.' Elena paused, choosing her words carefully. 'It's refreshing to work with someone who understands that farming is about stewardship, not just production.'

Pride warmed Guy. 'Dad instilled that in us from an early age. The land doesn't belong to us—we belong to it.'

'Exactly,' Elena said, her voice warm with approval. 'That's why I think your family will be successful with the changes I'm proposing. You have the right philosophy.'

'We just have to convince him,' Guy said.

They'd reached the farmhouse, where the sound of voices and the aroma of bacon drifted from the kitchen. Elena paused at the bottom of the porch steps, her expression thoughtful.

'Guy,' she said, 'I hope you don't mind me asking, but have you ever considered working outside Australia? Your approach to sustainable farming... there are operations around the world that could benefit from your expertise.'

The question caught Guy off guard. 'I've never really thought about it,' he said honestly. 'This farm has been my whole world since I was old enough to walk the rows with Dad. It's always been expected that I'll take over one day, like Dad did from my grandfather.'

Elena nodded, but something in her expression suggested that her suggestion was serious. Before Guy could pursue the thought, Amelia's voice carried through the screen door.

'Are you two planning to stand out there all morning discussing soil composition? Because the scrambled eggs are getting cold, and I have to go to work. The sooner Mum's home, the better.'

Elena laughed, a sound that never failed to

brighten Guy's mood. 'We'd better go in. We don't want to upset Amelia.'

'You're right. I have a bossy sister.'

Breakfast at the Johnson farmhouse was a boisterous affair. Oliver had joined them, full of enthusiasm about the weekend market plans with Sarah, while Amelia held court from her position at the stove, dispensing eggs and instructions. The two new seasonal workers, Ben and Marcus, looked slightly overwhelmed by the organised chaos that passed for normal conversation in the Johnson household.

'Elena, you must try Mum's chilli jam,' Amelia was saying as she loaded plates with scrambled eggs and bacon. 'She brought back some French techniques from their trip, and the strawberry-chilli batch is divine.'

'I'd love to,' Elena replied, accepting a plate that contained enough food to fuel a small army. 'In Brazil, my grandmother makes guava jam from a recipe that's been in our family for four generations. Perhaps I could share the recipe?'

'Oh, please!' Amelia's eyes lit up with the enthusiasm she usually reserved for her hair colour. 'I'm always looking for new preserving techniques.'

Guy watched the easy interaction between his sister and Elena, noting how naturally Elena fit into the family dynamic. Not many people understood Amelia so quickly.

She listened attentively to Oliver's market stories, asked thoughtful questions about Amelia's work at the preschool, and somehow managed to include Ben and Marcus in conversations that might otherwise have left them feeling like outsiders.

'So, what's the plan for today?' Oliver asked, reaching for the said chilli jam. 'Besides terrorising the eastern paddock with soil samples?'

'We want to map out potential locations for Elena's collection basin system,' Guy explained. 'Then run some calculations on implementation costs and timelines.'

'Sounds technical,' Ben observed, though his tone suggested interest rather than complaint. 'Mind if Marcus and I tag along? Always good to learn new techniques.'

Elena glanced at Guy, who nodded his

approval. 'Of course. The more perspectives we have, the better the final design will be.'

'Excellent,' Amelia declared, refilling coffee mugs with characteristic efficiency. 'A proper farm consultation. Very official.' She shot Guy a meaningful look that he chose to ignore.

After breakfast, the work party assembled in the eastern paddock with an assortment of measuring tools and notebooks. The morning had warmed considerably, but the autumn air still carried a crisp edge that made outdoor work pleasant.

Elena proved to be an excellent teacher, explaining her concepts clearly and encouraging questions from Ben and Marcus. Guy found himself watching her more than the land they were surveying—the way she gestured when she spoke, how her eyes lit up when someone grasped a particularly complex point, the unconscious grace with which she moved across the uneven ground.

'The key is working with the natural patterns rather than against them,' Elena was explaining as they stood at the highest point of the paddock.

Guy caught himself focusing more on the musical quality of her accent than the technical details, the way certain words carried the faint trace of her Portuguese heritage.

Marcus asked a technical question that Guy should have been following, but he was distracted by the animation on Elena's face. Her hands moved as she explained, and Guy found himself imagining what those hands might feel like.

'What do you think, Guy?' Elena asked suddenly, and he realised he'd been caught out.

'Sorry,' he said, feeling heat rise in his cheeks. 'Could you run through that last part again?'

Elena's smile suggested she knew exactly where his attention had been. 'Of course,' she said, but there was a warmth in her voice that hadn't been there when she was talking to the others.

As the morning progressed, Guy became increasingly aware of the small moments between them. When Elena needed to steady herself on the uneven ground, her hand briefly touched his arm. When she leaned close to show him something on her diagram, he caught the scent of her coconut shampoo. When she laughed at something Marcus said, her eyes sought Guy's first, as if his reaction mattered most.

Ben and Marcus seemed oblivious to the undercurrent of the interaction, focused entirely on the technical aspects of the project. But Guy felt it in every glance—the way Elena's gaze lingered on him a fraction longer than necessary, how she positioned herself slightly closer to him when the group clustered around her diagrams, the soft tone of her voice when she addressed him directly.

By noon, they'd gathered the data Elena needed, but Guy was conscious of time slipping away.

'I think we've got enough information to put together a proper proposal,' she said as they packed up their equipment. 'I can have preliminary designs ready by tomorrow evening, if you'd like to review them.'

The suggestion hung between them, and Guy wondered if he was reading too much into a simple professional courtesy.

'That would be perfect,' Guy replied, then found himself adding, 'Would you like to come to dinner tomorrow night? The whole family will be there—Mum and Dad will be back from the city, and my grandparents will be there.'

Elena's smile disappeared, and Guy caught a flicker of uncertainty before she answered. 'If you are sure I won't be intruding.'

'Of course not. They'd love to meet you.'

As they walked back towards the farmhouse, Ben and Marcus chatted about the morning's work, while Guy wondered what had caused that moment of hesitation. Did she think he was being pushy? Was he imagining her interest?

Or was she, like him, beginning to realise that their professional relationship was heading into the personal?

***

That evening, Elena sat in her cabin with her laptop open, ostensibly working on the drainage designs she'd promised Guy. But her attention kept drifting to the email from her father that remained unanswered in her inbox, and to the invitation to dinner with Guy's family that somehow felt more significant than a simple meal.

She'd been travelling for three years, working on farms across Australia, learning techniques and gathering experience to take back to Brazil. In all that time, she'd maintained professional relationships with her employers— friendly but with boundaries, useful but temporary. The Johnson farm shouldn't be any different.

But it was.

Guy filled her thoughts. His quiet intensity as he'd studied her diagrams, the way his entire face transformed when he smiled, the careful consideration he gave to every suggestion she made. She thought about the easy warmth of the Johnson siblings, the way they'd included her in their breakfast conversation as if she belonged there.

Most dangerously, she found herself wondering what it would be like to stay.

Elena closed her laptop with a decisive snap. She had three months to complete her research and return to Brazil, where a coffee farm and a family legacy were waiting for her. Whatever feelings were developing between her and Guy

Johnson, they had no future beyond the upcoming harvest season.

She would design his drainage system, share her expertise, and then return home to the responsibilities that had been defining her life since childhood. It was the sensible thing to do, the responsible choice.

So why did the prospect feel so much like walking away from something she wanted? Then she opened her laptop again and returned to her drainage calculations, pushing that dangerous thought back into the corners of her mind where it belonged.

Chapter 4

The Johnson family dinner table had been extended with an extra leaf to accommodate everyone—Elena, and the full complement of family members who had gathered to meet their newest consultant. Hugo and Ellen Johnson had returned from Brisbane and sat at either end of the long table, with *Grandmère* and Papa positioned where they could hold court over the assembled crowd. Charlotte and Greg were on the opposite side of the table with Julien and Emily beside them. Guy was pleased to be sitting opposite Elena, where he could look at her without being too obvious.

'If only Lisette would come home.' *Grandmère* put her hand to her forehead in a theatrical gesture. 'My cup would overflow.'

'Don't worry, *Grandmère*. If Lisette comes home, I'm sure your cup will be the least of what's overflowing. Try the laundry basket and the drama levels.'

Elena raised her eyebrows as she held Guy's eyes across the table. 'Who is that?' she mouthed.

'Another sister,' he said quietly. His response was lost in the many conversations going on around them. Elena held his eyes, and for a moment, it was as though they were the only ones at the table. She had changed into a flowing dress in burnished orange, her dark hair loose around her shoulders for once, instead of pulled back in its usual practical braid. Guy found it difficult to concentrate on anything other than how the soft fabric moved when she gestured, how the candlelight caught the gold flecks in her dark eyes.

'So, Elena,' his father said as he carved the roast, 'Guy tells me you've got some interesting ideas about our water management systems.'

'I hope so, Mr Johnson,' Elena replied, accepting a plate from Ellen. 'Your farm has an excellent base—solid infrastructure and sustainable practices. My suggestions are just refinements to build on what you've already established.'

Guy held his breath. Dad was notoriously difficult to impress, especially when it came to suggested changes to his farming methods. But

Elena's respectful acknowledgment of existing systems seemed to strike the right note.

'Call me Hugo, please,' he said. As his father settled back into his chair, Guy noticed how tired he looked. There had been no reason given for the trip to Brisbane, but he suspected it may have been a medical appointment.

'I'd like to hear more about these refinements,' his father said. 'Guy mentioned something about collection basins?'

Elena launched into an explanation of her drainage concepts, her enthusiasm evident but tempered with the kind of practical considerations that would appeal to Hugo's conservative approach. Guy watched his father sit up and take notice. His expression shifted from polite interest to genuine engagement as Elena described implementation phases and cost projections.

'In Brazil,' Elena was saying, 'we learned that gradual implementation is often more successful than dramatic overhauls. You can test each phase, adjust as needed, and spread the investment over multiple seasons.'

'Sensible approach,' Hugo nodded

approvingly. 'Too many consultants come in here wanting to rebuild everything from scratch.'

Grandmère, who had been listening with the sharp attention she usually reserved for family gossip, suddenly spoke up. '*Très intéressant*,' she declared. 'In my village in France, we had similar problems with water management. My cousin Antoine, he developed a system for the vineyards—very clever, very efficient. He showed us when we were there.'

Elena's face lit up with interest. 'I'd love to hear about that. Water management in wine country would have some unique challenges.'

What followed was an animated discussion between Elena and *Grandmère* about agricultural techniques across different continents, with Elena asking thoughtful questions about French methods and *Grandmère* delighting in having such an attentive audience for her stories.

'She's good,' Amelia murmured to Guy during a pause in the conversation. 'Knows exactly how to handle family dynamics.'

Guy glanced at his sister, noting the speculative gleam in her eyes. 'It's not manipulation, Amelia. Elana is genuinely interested in what people have to say.'

'I know that,' Amelia replied with a grin. 'That's what makes her perfect for you. You've always been attracted to substance over style.'

Before Guy could respond to that loaded statement, Oliver called for attention from his end of the table.

'Since we're all here,' he announced. 'I have some news to share.'

The table fell silent, all eyes turning to Oliver and the empty chair beside him where Sarah would have been sitting if she hadn't stayed home with Jett, who had a heavy head cold.

'Sarah and I have decided to make things official,' Oliver continued, his face splitting into a grin that transformed his usually serious expression. 'Sarah's agreed to move to the farm permanently. We're going to build a house on the northern boundary, near the creek. Oh, and as well as that, we're getting married.'

The eruption of congratulations and questions that followed threatened to overwhelm the dining room. Ellen burst into tears of joy,

Hugo stood to shake Oliver's hand with gruff pride, and *Grandmère* immediately began planning celebration menus in rapid-fire French.

'*Trois mariages*,' she said

Guy's feelings were mixed as he watched his brother field questions about wedding plans and house construction. Joy for Oliver's happiness, certainly, but also a sharp awareness of the contrast between his brother's settled future and his uncertain one. 'That's wonderful news,' Elena said warmly when the initial excitement had died down. 'Sarah seems like a lovely woman, and Jett sounds delightful.'

'You'll have to meet him soon,' Oliver replied. 'He's been asking about the Brazilian lady who knows about farming. He's heard everyone talking about you.'

Guy watched as a pretty blush spread across Elena's cheeks at Oliver's words, the colour rising from her neck to bloom across her face in a way that made his chest tighten. She ducked her head slightly, a small smile playing at the corners of her mouth, and Guy felt something shift inside him—a pull so strong it nearly took his breath away.

He wished desperately that they were alone. The dinner conversation continued around them, but all Guy could focus on was the soft curve of Elena's mouth, the way her eyelashes cast shadows on her flushed cheeks, the graceful line of her neck. The overwhelming desire to lean across the table and kiss her hit him with such force that he had to grip his wine glass to keep his hands steady.

She looked up then, catching his intense gaze, and for a moment the rest of the family seemed to fade away. Her lips parted slightly, and Guy wondered if she could read everything he was thinking from his expression. The air between them felt charged, electric.

'Guy?' Amelia's voice cut through his daze. 'Are you listening to me?'

He blinked, forcing himself back to the present, though Elena's blush had deepened and she was now very carefully not looking at him.

'Sorry. I missed that,' he said. 'What's up?'

Amelia rolled her eyes and then grinned at *Grandmère,* who was looking at him with a crafty look on her face.

No, please. That was all he needed.

Grandmère and Amelia ganging up on him.

As the evening progressed, he smiled as Elena listened attentively to Papa's stories about the cane farming techniques of his youth, offered practical suggestions when *Grandmère* mentioned her struggles with her new herb garden, and somehow managed to make both Ben and Marcus feel included in conversations that might otherwise have left them as observers.

But it was her interaction with his parents that impressed Guy most. Elena showed genuine respect for Dad's explanations while gently introducing concepts that challenged traditional approaches. She asked Mum about family recipes and showed interest in family traditions.

'Elena,' Ellen said as she cleared the dinner plates, 'Guy mentioned you're planning to return to Brazil during harvest. Will you be taking over your family's farm then?'

'That's the plan,' Elena replied, though Guy thought he detected a note of uncertainty in her voice. 'It's been in my family for five generations. My father's ready to retire, and my brothers have other careers, so the responsibility falls to me.'

'That's quite a burden for someone your age,' Hugo observed.

Elena's smile was slightly strained. 'It's an honour, really. The farm has tremendous potential for growth and modernisation. The techniques I've learned in Australia will help transform our operation.'

'But?' *Grandmère* prompted with the shrewd perception that came from eight decades of reading people.

Elena glanced around the table, her gaze lingering on Guy before she answered. 'But sometimes I wonder if I'm ready for such a big responsibility. Running a farm that size, managing workers—it's intimidating.'

'You'll be fine,' Guy said quietly, his voice carrying absolute conviction. 'I've seen how you work, how you think through problems. Your family's lucky to have you.'

Something passed between them as she held his eyes—a moment of connection that caused Guy's pulse to quicken. It was Amelia who broke the spell by standing to serve dessert, her knowing smile suggesting she'd seen their shared look.

'Who's on for bread-and-butter pudding?'

After dinner, Guy walked Elena to her car; she'd driven the short distance to the farmhouse, in case the forecast rain arrived, but the sky was clear, with a brilliant canopy of stars visible. Ben and Marcus opted to walk.

'Thank you for inviting me to dinner,' Elena said as Guy stood with her. 'Your family is wonderful. I can see where you get your approach to farming—that combination of innovation and respect for tradition.'

'They liked you,' Guy replied. 'Dad doesn't usually engage that much with consultants. And *Grandmère* practically adopted you.'

Elena laughed softly. 'She reminds me of my grandmother. Same sharp eyes, same ability to see straight through people's polite facades.'

'What did she see when she looked at you?' Guy asked, moving closer as Elena put her hand on the open door.

She met his gaze directly, and Guy saw uncertainty in her expression. 'Someone who's not as sure about her path as she pretends to be.'

He stepped closer.

'Elena,' he began, her name barely more

than a whisper, then stopped. How could he possibly put into words the way she'd turned his carefully ordered world upside down in just a few days? How could he explain that every moment since she'd arrived, he'd felt more alive than anything he'd experienced in years?

She didn't step back as he moved another step closer, and in the moonlight, he could see her eyes searching his face. The space between them hummed with possibility, with all the things they hadn't said, all the careful professional boundaries they'd been dancing around since that first moment in the kitchen.

'I don't know what this is,' he said finally, his voice rough with honesty. 'I just know that when you leave, I'm going to miss you.'

Elena's expression softened, and she took a small step closer, close enough that he could catch the faint scent of her citrus perfume mixed with the night air.

'Guy,' she said quietly. 'I know,' she said softly. 'I feel it too. But...'

'But you're leaving in three months,' he finished for her.

'But I'm leaving in three months,' she

confirmed, her voice barely above a whisper.

Guy reached out, gently touching her cheek with the back of his hand. Elena leaned into the contact for just a moment before stepping back.

'I should go,' she said, fishing her keys from her bag with hands that weren't quite steady. 'Early start tomorrow.'

'Elena,' Guy called as she opened the driver's door. When she looked back, he found himself asking the question that had been haunting him since her first day back. 'What if you didn't have to choose? Between going home and…?'

Elena's expression grew pained. 'But I do have to choose, Guy. My family, my responsibilities—they're not negotiable.'

***

Elena's hands were shaking as she parked outside her cabin. The evening had been wonderful—too wonderful. The warmth of Guy's family, the easy way they'd all accepted her, the way Guy himself had looked at her across the dinner table—it all painted a picture of a life she would love.

But wanting something and being able to

have it were two very different things.

Her phone buzzed with a text message from her father, and she pulled a face as she read it: **Coffee market prices improving. Good time to expand production. Looking forward to your return and implementation of new techniques.**

Elena stared at the message. Her father had sacrificed his dreams to keep the family farm running. Her grandfather had done the same, and his father before him. Five generations of Santiagos had built something meaningful in the hills of Brazil, and now it was her turn to carry that legacy forward.

But as she looked towards the warm lights of the Johnson farmhouse, Elena knew she would be walking away from something equally meaningful.

Chapter 5

Guy had been up since dawn, ostensibly checking irrigation lines but really just finding excuses to be out in the paddock when Elena came out. The conversation from the night before had replayed in his mind countless times, along with the memory of her face when he'd asked about choosing between her responsibilities and... whatever this was between them.

Elena emerged from her car in work clothes and practical boots, but Guy's trained eye noticed the slight shadows under her eyes that suggested she'd slept as poorly as he had. She carried her ever-present notes and a thermos that probably contained the strong Brazilian coffee she favoured.

'Morning,' she called, her voice determinedly cheerful. 'Ready to get our hands dirty with soil composition analysis?'

'Always,' Guy replied, falling into step beside her as they headed towards the paddock. 'Sleep well?'

Elena's pause was barely perceptible. 'Well enough. I spent some time working on the detailed schematics for your drainage system. I think you'll be pleased with the modifications.'

They were back to professional mode, Guy realised. Whatever vulnerability she'd shown the night before was now carefully packed away behind her consultant persona. He told himself it was probably for the best, but the careful distance in her voice left him feeling oddly bereft.

Ben and Marcus were early too, already waiting by the equipment shed, eager to continue their education in sustainable water management. Elena threw herself into the teaching role with perhaps more enthusiasm than strictly necessary, explaining soil percolation rates and drainage coefficients with the kind of detailed focus that left no room for personal conversation.

'The key thing to remember,' she was telling Ben as they worked their way through a series of test holes, 'is that different soil compositions require different approaches. Clay content, organic matter, subsurface rock formations—

they all affect how water moves through the system.'

Guy found himself watching her hands as she demonstrated proper soil sampling techniques. She had beautiful hands—strong and capable, with long fingers that moved with precision whether she was testing soil consistency or sketching drainage patterns.

'Guy?' Marcus's voice broke through his distraction. 'Elena asked if you wanted to review the percolation results from the northern test site.'

Heat crept up Guy's neck as he realised he'd been caught staring. 'Sorry. Yes, let's have a look.'

Elena's expression was carefully neutral as she handed him the clipboard containing their measurements, but Guy caught a flicker of awareness that suggested she'd noticed his inattention. Their fingers brushed as he took the clipboard, and he felt that familiar jolt of connection that seemed to occur whenever they touched.

The morning's work progressed efficiently, with Elena maintaining her professional demeanour and Guy struggling to match it. By the time they broke for lunch, they'd gathered enough data to finalise the drainage system design, but the previous easy camaraderie had been replaced by a polite formality that felt worse than open conflict.

'I'll have the final schematics ready by this evening,' Elena announced as they packed up their equipment. 'If you'd like to review them before I submit the formal proposal.'

'Of course,' Guy replied, trying to read her expression. 'Same time as before?'

'Actually,' Elena said, not meeting his eyes, 'perhaps we could meet in the office this time. More professional setting for a business review. I'm going to go into town for lunch today.'

The suggestion hit Guy like a physical blow. The office was sterile and impersonal, nothing like the warm intimacy of the kitchen where they'd spread her diagrams just two nights ago. Elena was deliberately putting distance between them, and while Guy understood her reasoning, it didn't make the rejection any easier to accept.

'Whatever suits,' he managed to say evenly.

As Elena drove away for her lunch break,

Ben fell into step beside Guy as they walked towards the farmhouse.

'Elena seems different today,' the younger man observed. 'More... professional, I guess.'

Guy glanced at him sharply. 'What do you mean?'

'Yesterday she was joking with us, asking about our backgrounds, really friendly. Today it's all business.' Ben shrugged. 'Not complaining—she's still a great teacher. Just different.'

Marcus nodded in agreement as they reached the porch. 'Like she's got something on her mind. You notice anything, Guy?'

Guy had noticed plenty, but none of it was appropriate to discuss with the seasonal workers. 'Elena carries a lot of responsibility,' he said diplomatically. 'Probably just focused on getting the project completed properly.'

The day passed quickly, and after dinner, he made his way to the office, which had been designed by Papa, who prioritised function over comfort. A large desk dominated the small room, surrounded by filing cabinets and shelves crammed with farming manuals, weather records, and equipment catalogues that never were thrown out. The overhead fluorescent light cast everything in harsh, clinical brightness that made the space feel more like a medical examination room than a place for collaboration. Guy was embarrassed as he looked at the office and saw how it would look to someone else. He smoothed his hands down the front of his clean shirt as he heard Elena's car pull up outside precisely at eight o'clock.

***

Elena was armed with her completed schematics and a determination to keep their meeting strictly professional. After her lunch trip to town, she'd spent the afternoon working on the diagrams with almost desperate focus, using the technical demands of the project to avoid thinking about Guy's question from the night before.

What if you didn't have to choose?

But she did have to choose.

The fact that she was increasingly tempted to abandon all of that for a man she'd known for less than two seasons only proved how dangerous this situation had become.

'These are impressive,' Guy said, studying the detailed schematics she'd spread across the desk. 'You've thought of everything—installation phases, cost projections, maintenance schedules.'

Elena forced herself to focus on the technical discussion, pointing out key features and explaining her reasoning for various design choices. But she was acutely aware of Guy's proximity in the small, cluttered study, the way his shoulder occasionally brushed hers as they leaned over the drawings, the subtle scent of soap and sunshine that seemed to cling to his clothes.

'The initial investment is significant,' she admitted, 'but the long-term water savings should offset the costs within three seasons.'

Guy nodded, making notes in the margins of her drawings. 'Dad will want to see the numbers broken down by phase. He's more comfortable with gradual implementation than major capital expenditures.'

'Of course. I can have a detailed financial analysis ready by tomorrow.' Elena began gathering her materials, eager to escape the confines of the small room and Guy's unsettling presence. 'If there are no other questions...'

'Elena, wait.' Guy's voice stopped her as she reached for the door handle. 'About last night—'

'Last night was a mistake,' Elena interrupted, not turning around. 'I shouldn't have... we shouldn't have...'

'Shouldn't have what?' Guy asked quietly. 'Talked honestly about what we're both feeling?'

Elena's hand tightened on the door handle. 'We shouldn't have complicated a professional relationship with personal feelings.'

'Is that what we're doing? Complicating things?'

Elena finally turned to face him, her expression carefully composed despite the turmoil she felt inside. 'Yes, Guy. That's exactly what we're doing. And I can't afford complications right now.'

Guy studied her face for a long moment, and Elena had the uncomfortable feeling that he could see right through her professional facade to the uncertainty beneath.

'What are you so afraid of?' he asked finally.

The question caught Elena off guard. 'I'm not afraid—'

'You are,' Guy interrupted gently. 'You're terrified that if you allow yourself to consider alternatives, you might choose something different than what everyone expects from you.'

Elena's carefully constructed composure began to crack. 'You don't understand—'

'Don't I?' Guy stepped closer, his voice soft but intense. 'I've been the responsible son my entire life, Elena. The one who stays on the farm while his siblings pursue their own dreams. The one who puts family obligations ahead of personal desires. I understand exactly what you're feeling.'

'Then you understand why this has to stay professional,' Elena replied, her voice barely steady. 'I have responsibilities, Guy. People depending on me.'

'And what about what you want?' Guy asked. 'What about your happiness?'

Elena's composure finally shattered. 'What I want doesn't matter!' The words came out more forcefully than she'd intended, driven by months of suppressed frustration and uncertainty. 'Do you think I haven't thought about alternatives? Do you think I don't wonder what it would be like to choose my own path for once?'

Guy reached for her, but Elena stepped back, creating physical distance to match the emotional barriers she was trying to rebuild.

'But wondering doesn't change reality,' she continued, her voice quieter now but no less intense. 'My father sacrificed his dream of being an architect to keep our farm running, and now it's my turn.'

'What if there was another way?' Guy asked. 'What if you could fulfil your family obligations and still have a life of your own?'

Elena shook her head, tears threatening despite her efforts to maintain control. 'There isn't another way, Guy. My family's farm is in Brazil. My responsibilities are there. And you... you belong here, with your family, with this land.'

'People can change their minds about where they belong,' Guy said quietly.

Elena didn't dare examine his suggestion too closely. For just a moment, she allowed herself to imagine what it might be like—Guy in Brazil, working alongside her to transform her family's farm, bringing his quiet strength and innovative thinking to bear on challenges an ocean away from everything he'd ever known.

Then reality reasserted itself, and Elena forced herself to remember all the reasons why such dreams were impossible.

'I should go,' she said, reaching for the door handle again. 'Thank you for reviewing the schematics. I'll have the financial analysis ready tomorrow.'

This time, Guy didn't try to stop her as she left, but Elena could feel his gaze following her as she walked away quickly. Only when she was safely inside her cabin did she allow the tears to fall.

Chapter 6

Guy stood at his bedroom window, watching the cane fields emerge from pre-dawn darkness. Three days had passed since his conversation with Elena in the office, and she'd maintained her strictly professional distance with determination that was as impressive as it was frustrating. She completed her tasks efficiently, answered his questions with accuracy, and managed to avoid being alone with him through a series of manoeuvres that would have been admirable if they weren't slowly driving him mad.

The financial analysis she'd promised had been delivered via Ben, who'd seemed puzzled by the formal handoff but had dutifully carried the folder to Guy's desk. The numbers were impressive—Elena's drainage system would pay for itself within three seasons and generate significant long-term savings. Dad had been sufficiently convinced to approve the first phase of implementation, starting after harvest.

But Guy found himself caring less about

water management efficiency and more about the careful way Elena avoided his eyes during their daily briefings, the professional smile she wore like armour, the deliberate distance she maintained whenever they worked together.

He missed *her*.

The realisation had crept up on him gradually, but now it sat in his chest like a physical ache. He missed her laugh, her animated explanations of farming techniques, the way her face lit up when she understood a new concept. He missed the Elena who had spread her diagrams across his kitchen table and talked about her dreams for her family's farm with passionate intensity.

A soft knock on his bedroom door interrupted his brooding. 'Guy?' Amelia's voice was uncharacteristically subdued. 'Can I come in?'

'It's open.'

Amelia entered carrying two mugs of coffee, her burgundy hair tousled from sleep and her expression unusually serious. She handed him one of the mugs and settled cross-legged on his bed, regarding him with the shrewd attention she usually reserved for her more dramatic crises.

'You look terrible,' she announced without preamble.

'Good morning to you too,' Guy replied, accepting the coffee gratefully. 'What's so urgent it couldn't wait until breakfast?'

'Elena's leaving.'

Guy nearly dropped his mug. 'What do you mean, leaving? Her contract runs through harvest—'

'Not leaving leaving,' Amelia clarified quickly. 'But she asked Dad about accelerating the drainage project timeline. Something about wanting to see the first phase completed before she returns to Brazil.'

Guy felt something cold settle in his stomach. 'That would mean...?'

'Working seven-day weeks, pushing the installation crews to their limits, probably finishing everything by the end of next month instead of spread over the entire season, Dad said.' Amelia studied her brother's face. 'She wants to leave early, Guy. And I think we both know it's not because she's eager to get back to Brazil.'

Guy stared into his coffee, processing this information. Elena was running—from him, from the temptation that threatened her carefully planned future. He should probably respect her decision, let her complete her work and return to her responsibilities without interference.

Instead, he found himself thinking about Oliver's pursuit of Sarah, about the patience and persistence his brother had shown in winning over the woman who had transformed his life.

'What are you going to do about it?' Amelia asked, as if reading his thoughts.

'Nothing,' Guy said automatically. 'Elena's made her choice. I'm not going to pressure her into something she doesn't want.'

Amelia snorted inelegantly. 'Oh, please. The woman's practically vibrating with suppressed lust every time she looks at you. This isn't about not wanting something—it's about being too scared to reach for it.'

'You don't understand—'

'I understand plenty,' Amelia interrupted. 'I understand that Elena Santiago is the first woman who's ever made you question whether the farm is enough. I understand that you've been moping around here for three days like a lovesick teenager. And I know that if you let her walk away without fighting for her, you'll regret it for the rest of your life.'

'When did you grow up and get so wise?' Guy looked at his sister, noting the fierce protectiveness in her expression. For all her dramatics and interference, Amelia genuinely wanted him to be happy.

'Even if I wanted to fight for Elena,' he said quietly, 'what would that look like? She has responsibilities in Brazil, family obligations. I can't ask her to abandon all of that for... what? A seasonal romance that might not survive the reality of daily life?'

'You're right,' Amelia said, setting down her mug with decisive precision. 'You can't ask her to abandon her responsibilities. But maybe you could ask her to share them.'

Guy stared at her. 'What do you mean?'

'I mean maybe the solution isn't Elena staying here or you staying here. Maybe it's you going there.'

The suggestion hit Guy like a physical blow. Leave Australia? Leave the farm that had been his entire world since childhood? The idea was so foreign, so impossible, that he couldn't even begin to process it.

'I can't leave,' he said automatically. 'The farm needs—'

'The farm needs capable management,' Amelia corrected. 'It doesn't specifically need you. Oliver's here, I'm here, we could hire additional help. Dad's not ready to retire, but he's certainly capable of managing operations with support.'

The walls of Guy's carefully ordered world shifted around him. 'You're talking about me permanently relocating to Brazil. Leaving everything I've ever known.'

'I'm talking about you considering whether the life you've always planned is really the life you want,' Amelia replied gently. 'Elena's not the only one who's dealing with expectations, Guy. When's the last time you thought about what would make you happy, not what the farm needs or what the family expects?'

The question echoed the one he'd asked Elena just days before, and Guy felt a flash of understanding about why she'd reacted so strongly. When you'd spent your entire life defining yourself through duty, the concept of personal happiness could feel like a foreign language.

'I need to think about this,' he said finally.

Amelia smiled. 'Good. Think fast, though. Elena's planning to finish her work here within the month, and once she's back in Brazil...'

She didn't need to finish the sentence. They both knew that once Elena returned to her family's farm, any change of plans would be much more difficult.

After Amelia left, Guy remained at his window. For the first time in his adult life, he allowed himself to imagine a future that didn't centre on this farm, this land, this carefully planned existence.

The image that formed in his mind was both terrifying and exhilarating: rolling hills covered in coffee plants as well as sugar cane, a different kind of farming in a different hemisphere, Elena beside him as they worked to transform her family's operation using the techniques they'd developed together.

It was a dream so far outside his experience

that he didn't even know how to begin to make it reality. But as Guy finally headed downstairs for breakfast, he knew he had to talk to Elena, and tell her how he felt.

***

Elena stood in the middle of the paddock near the house trying to find some peace in the familiar rhythm of agricultural work. The morning was warm but not yet oppressive, with a light breeze carrying the scent of growing cane and rich earth. Under other circumstances, it would have been a perfect working day.

Instead, she felt like she was slowly coming apart, pulled between the professional task that had brought her here and her feelings for Guy that threatened to derail everything she'd planned for her future.

The accelerated timeline she'd requested from Hugo Johnson had been approved, along with additional labour to ensure the drainage project could be completed within four weeks instead of spread over the entire harvest season. It was a practical solution that would allow her to return to Brazil early, before the situation with Guy became any more complicated than it already was. Guilt churned in her; she'd been too much of a coward to tell him what she'd asked for.

'Elena?' Marcus's voice interrupted her thoughts. 'Guy's looking for you. Says he needs to review the installation sequence for the collection basins. He's in the machinery shed.'

Elena's pulse quickened despite her efforts to maintain professional composure. Over the past three days, Guy had respected her desire for distance, communicating through the other workers when possible and keeping their direct interactions brief and task-focused. If he was seeking her out now, it probably meant a genuine work issue that required her expertise.

Or it meant he was as tired of the artificial barriers between them as she was.

'Tell him I'll be there in ten minutes,' she replied, packing up her soil samples with hands that weren't quite steady. 'I just need to finish this moisture assessment.'

Marcus nodded and jogged back towards the farmhouse, leaving Elena alone with her racing thoughts. She could handle this, she told herself. One more professional conversation, focused on technical details and implementation logistics. Then she could return to her cabin and continue the work of convincing herself that leaving early was the right decision.

But when she approached the machinery shed where Guy was waiting, her composure begin to waver. He stood with his back to her, studying the irrigation maps they'd drawn up together, his posture tense in a way that suggested he was struggling with his own internal conflicts.

'Marcus said you needed to review the installation sequence,' she said, proud of how steady her voice sounded.

Guy turned, and Elena saw immediately that this wasn't going to be a routine technical discussion. His expression held a determination she'd never seen before, along with something that might have been fear.

'I've been thinking about what you said,' he began without preamble. 'About responsibilities and family obligations and not having a choice.'

Elena felt her heart begin to race. 'Guy, I thought we agreed—'

'We didn't agree on anything,' Guy

interrupted gently. 'You ran away before we could have a real conversation about what we're both feeling.'

'I didn't run away,' Elena protested, though they both knew it wasn't entirely true. 'I chose to maintain professional boundaries.'

'Professional boundaries,' Guy repeated, as if testing the phrase. 'Is that what we're calling it?'

Elena lifted her chin, drawing on every reserve of strength she possessed. 'That's what it is. I'm here to complete a consulting project, and then I'm returning to Brazil to take over my family's farm. They're looking at the water management as part of a study.. Anything beyond that is just... too complicated.'

Guy stepped closer, and Elena forced herself not to retreat. 'What if complications aren't necessarily bad things?' he asked. 'What if they're just opportunities we haven't figured out how to navigate yet?'

Elena's voice shook. 'What are you suggesting, Guy?'

'I'm suggesting that maybe there's a third option we haven't considered.' Guy's voice was quiet but intense. 'You're right that your family needs you, that the farm is your responsibility. But what if you didn't have to handle that responsibility alone?'

Elena stared at him, afraid to hope she understood what he was suggesting. 'What do you mean?'

Guy took a deep breath, and Elena could see him gathering courage for whatever he was about to say. 'I mean what if I came with you? To Brazil?'

The words hit Elena like a physical blow. She'd allowed herself to imagine many scenarios over the past weeks, but Guy voluntarily leaving his family's farm to join her in Brazil hadn't been one of them.

'You can't be serious,' she whispered.

'I've never been more serious about anything in my life,' Guy replied. 'Elena, I know it sounds crazy, but think about it. Your family's farm needs modernisation and sustainable practices—exactly the kind of work I've been doing here. My knowledge of Australian techniques combined with your understanding of Brazilian conditions could transform your operation. We could try it and give these feeling between us a chance to work. Couldn't we?'

Elena's eyes ached with threatening tears, overwhelmed by the magnitude of what he was offering. 'Guy, you don't understand what you're saying. Your entire life is here—your family, your farm, everything you've ever known.'

'My entire life has been about duty and obligation,' Guy corrected. 'About being the responsible son who never questions other possibilities. But these past weeks with you... Elena, you've shown me that maybe there's more to life than just maintaining what already exists.'

Elena shook her head, unable to process the emotions flooding through her. 'You can't abandon your family's farm for me. That's not fair to anyone. We haven't even tested how we feel and you're talking about crossing the ocean with me?'

'I'm not abandoning anything,' Guy said, his voice growing stronger with conviction. 'I'm choosing to expand my definition of what family and responsibility mean. Oliver's here, Amelia's here, my parents are nowhere near ready to retire. The farm will be fine without me.'

'But you love this place,' Elena protested, gesturing towards the fields that stretched around them. 'This land is part of who you are.'

Guy smiled, and Elena felt her heart skip at the warmth in his expression. 'This land taught me how to farm, how to work with natural systems instead of against them. But it's not the only place where those lessons apply. And...' He paused, reaching out to gently touch her cheek. 'I want you to be a part of who I am too.'

Elena leaned into his touch for just a moment before stepping back, overwhelmed by the implications of what he was offering. 'I need to think about this,' she said, her voice barely above a whisper.

'Think about it,' Guy agreed. 'But Elena? Don't think so hard that you convince yourself it's impossible. Sometimes the best ideas are the ones that seem crazy at first.'

As Elena walked back to her cabin, her mind spinning, Guy's expression when he'd offered to follow her to Brazil—determination mixed with vulnerability—was all she could see.

For the first time in her life Elena allowed herself to truly consider what it might mean to choose her own happiness alongside her family responsibilities. The prospect was both terrifying and exhilarating.

But as she reached her cabin and saw the latest email from her father waiting on her laptop screen—another reminder of equipment installations and expansion plans that depended on her return—Elena was forced to confront the reality that wanting something and being able to have it were still two very different things.

The question now was whether she had the courage to find out if Guy's impossible suggestion might somehow become possible after all.

Chapter 7

Elena stared at her laptop screen, the cursor blinking mockingly in the empty email composition window she'd opened and closed at least a dozen times over the past two hours.

Three days had passed since Guy's stunning proposal, and Elena had managed to avoid any meaningful conversation with him through a combination of early morning departures and late evening returns. But avoidance wasn't a strategy that would last, especially when every glimpse of him across the paddock sent her heart racing and her carefully planned arguments tumbling into chaos.

She needed perspective. She needed advice from someone who understood the family obligation. Most of all, she needed to hear her father's voice, even if she wasn't ready to tell him about Guy's offer.

Elena finally began typing:

Papai,

I hope this finds you and Mama well. The work here

in Australia continues to be productive—I've completed the drainage system design for the Johnson farm and overseen the beginning of implementation. The techniques I'm learning will be invaluable for our own expansion plans.

I've been thinking about our conversation before I left, about the responsibility of carrying forward five generations of family legacy. You mentioned that Grandfather had doubts sometimes about the path chosen for him. I wonder... did you ever question whether the farm was truly what you wanted, or whether you simply accepted it as inevitable?

I ask because I find myself at a crossroads I didn't expect. The work here has opened my eyes to possibilities I hadn't considered, both professionally and personally. I know you're counting on my return, and I don't want to disappoint you or dishonour our family's sacrifices. But I also wonder if there might be ways to fulfil our obligations while also allowing for... unexpected opportunities.

Please give Mama my love. I hope to speak with you soon.

Com amor, Elena

She read the message three times before finding the courage to send it. The words felt inadequate to express the turmoil in her heart, but they were a beginning—a tentative step towards a conversation she'd been avoiding for far too long.

Elena's phone buzzed with a text message from Guy: **Working late again? The drainage calculations can wait until tomorrow.**

She looked out of her window; he was standing on the farmhouse porch, backlit by the warm glow spilling from the kitchen. Even at a distance, she could read the concern in his posture, the careful way he held himself as if prepared for rejection.

Before she could lose her nerve, Elena grabbed her jacket and headed outside.

Guy was still on the porch as she hurried through the gate to the back garden, though he'd settled into one of the weathered rocking chairs that looked as though they had been there for a long time. The evening air was crisp with the promise of winter, and overhead, the first stars were becoming visible in the darkening sky.

'I sent an email to my father,' Elena said without preamble, settling into the chair beside him.

Guy's expression remained carefully neutral. 'About the drainage project?'

'About choices,' Elena replied. 'About whether the path we think we have to follow is really the only option available.'

They sat in silence for a moment, the familiar sounds of the farm settling around them like a gentle embrace. Elena found herself studying Guy's profile in the dim light—the strong line of his jaw, the intense expression he wore when thinking a problem though, his quiet strength that had drawn her to him from the moment she met him.

'I keep thinking about what you said,' she continued. 'About coming to Brazil. Part of me wants to believe it could work, that we could find a way to honour my family's expectations while also... this.' She gestured between them, encompassing all the unnamed feelings that had been growing stronger with each passing day.

'But?' Guy prompted gently.

'But another part of me is terrified that I'm being selfish. That I'm using your offer as an excuse to avoid the difficult choices I know I need to make.' Elena turned to face him fully.

'Guy, what if you give up everything here and it doesn't work? What if the reality of running a coffee farm in Brazil is nothing like the fantasy we're imagining?'

Guy considered her question seriously before answering. 'What if it is exactly what we're imagining? What if it's even better?'

'You can't know that,' Elena protested. 'You've never even been to South America, let alone worked with coffee cultivation. The climate, the soil conditions, the labour practices—everything would be different from what you know here.'

'Everything except the fundamental principles,' Guy replied. 'Sustainable agriculture, water management, soil health—those concepts apply regardless of hemisphere. And Elena, I wouldn't be going blind into your world. I'd be going with you, learning from your expertise the same way you've been sharing yours with us.'

Elena felt her heart constrict at the quiet confidence in his voice. 'What about your family? Oliver and Amelia need you here. Your parents...'

'My family wants me to be happy,' Guy interrupted gently. 'Oliver's building his own life with Sarah, Amelia's discovering her own path—even if she's taking the scenic route to get there. And my parents... they survived raising six children with very different personalities and ambitions. They'll adapt to having one of those children choose an unexpected path.'

The conviction in his voice made Elena's breath catch. 'You've really thought about this.'

'I've thought about little else for the past three days,' Guy admitted. 'Elena, I know I'm asking you to take an enormous risk. I know that bringing me into your family's farm would complicate everything you've planned. But I also know that I've never felt about anyone the way I feel about you.'

Elena's pulse quickened at the admission. 'Guy...'

'I love you,' he said simply, the words carrying absolute certainty. 'I love your intelligence, your passion for agriculture, the way you see possibilities where others see only problems. I love how you explain concepts with patience and enthusiasm, how you listen to my family's stories as if they matter to you personally.'

Elena felt tears prick her eyes. 'It does matter to me. You all matter to me.'

'Then let me matter enough to take a chance on,' Guy said, reaching for her hand. 'Let me come to Brazil and learn your world the way you've learned mine. Let me help you transform your family's farm into something that respects the past while embracing the future.'

Elena stared down at their joined hands, overwhelmed by the magnitude of what he was offering. 'What if my father says no? What if he thinks bringing an Australian farmer into our operation is too risky?'

'Then we'll convince him together,' Guy replied. 'Elena, your father spent three years allowing you to gain experience across Australia because he recognised that innovation requires outside perspectives. I'm just another perspective—one that comes with a personal investment in your success.'

Elena found herself laughing despite the tears that threatened to spill over. 'You make it sound simple.'

'Maybe it is simple,' Guy suggested. 'Maybe we're the ones making it complicated by overthinking all the potential problems instead of focusing on the potential solutions.'

Elena looked into his face, seeing determination mixed with vulnerability, hope tempered by realism. This man was willing to leave everything familiar for the chance to build something new with her. The enormity of his offer was both humbling and terrifying.

'I need to talk to my father,' she said finally. 'Really talk to him, not just hint around the edges of what I'm thinking.'

Guy nodded, though she could see the effort it cost him to remain patient. 'When?'

'Tomorrow,' Elena decided, surprising herself with the certainty. 'I'll video call him tomorrow morning, before I lose my nerve.'

Guy squeezed her hand gently. 'Whatever he says, whatever you decide—I meant what I told you. I love you, Elena. That's not going to change regardless of geography.'

Elena felt her last defences crumble at the quiet sincerity in his voice. 'I love you too,' she whispered, the admission both liberation and commitment. 'I think I've been falling in love with you since the first time we worked together on irrigation plans.'

Guy's smile transformed his entire face, and Elena felt her heart skip at the joy she saw there. When he leaned forward to kiss her, she met him halfway, pouring all her hope and fear and desperate affection into the connection between them.

When they finally broke apart, both slightly breathless, Guy rested his forehead against hers. 'Whatever happens tomorrow, we'll figure it out together.'

Elena nodded, finally allowing herself to believe that maybe, just maybe, she could choose both love and duty.

Chapter 8

The video call to Brazil was scheduled for six o'clock in the morning Queensland time, which meant three o'clock in the afternoon for her father in São Paulo. Elena had been awake since four-thirty, pacing her small cabin and rehearsing conversations that she knew she wouldn't remember.

Guy had offered to be there for moral support, but Elena had declined, knowing this conversation needed to happen between her and her father without the complication of his presence. Still, the knowledge that Guy was waiting in the main house, ready to provide whatever support she needed, gave her the courage to finally dial home.

Miguel Santiago answered on the second ring, his weathered face filling the laptop screen with a warm smile that immediately reminded Elena of home. Behind him, she could see his familiar office—walls lined with certificates and photographs chronicling five generations of coffee cultivation, the massive window that overlooked the terraced hills where their livelihood grew.

'Elena, *minha filha*!' His voice carried genuine pleasure. 'How wonderful to see your face. You look well—the Australian air agrees with you.'

'*Oi, Papai*,' Elena replied, her throat tight with sudden emotion. 'You look well too. How are Mama and the boys?'

'All excellent. Carlos got the promotion he was hoping for at the bank, and Roberto's wife is expecting their second child in the spring. The family grows, even as you wander the world learning new tricks.'

Elena smiled, warmed by the family updates. But underneath her pleasure at seeing her father, anxiety churned like a physical obstruction. How did one tell a man who had sacrificed his own dreams for family obligation that his daughter was considering a path that had never been part of their plans?

'*Papai*,' she began carefully, 'I received your message about accelerating the timeline for my return. I wanted to discuss that with you.'

Miguel's expression grew more focused. 'Of

course. The new processing equipment is installed but not yet operational, and we have decisions to make about the expansion into the southern hills. Your expertise will be invaluable for both projects.'

'I understand the importance of those projects,' Elena said, choosing her words carefully. 'But I've been wondering... what if there was a way to approach them differently? With additional expertise, perhaps additional perspectives?'

Her father's eyebrows rose with interest. 'What do you mean?'

Elena took a deep breath, knowing there was no way to ease into what she needed to say. 'I mean bringing someone with me when I return. Someone with expertise in sustainable agriculture and water management systems that could transform our entire operation.'

'A consultant?' Miguel asked, though something in his expression suggested he sensed this wasn't a purely professional discussion.

'A partner,' Elena clarified, her heart racing. '*Papai*, I've met someone. An Australian farmer with extensive experience in exactly the kind of innovations we need to implement. He's... he's offered to come to Brazil with me, to help modernise our operation while learning coffee cultivation.'

The silence that followed felt endless. Elena watched her father's face carefully, trying to read his reaction through the pixelated connection. When he finally spoke, his voice was carefully controlled.

'This is very sudden, Elena.'

'I know it seems that way,' Elena rushed to explain. 'But *Papai*, the techniques he's developed here could revolutionise our water efficiency. The drainage systems, the soil management practices—we could increase our yield while reducing our environmental impact.'

'And this man,' Miguel said quietly, 'what are his qualifications beyond agricultural expertise?'

Elena felt heat rise in her cheeks. 'His name is Guy Johnson. His family has been farming in Queensland for three generations. He's intelligent, hardworking, and completely dedicated to sustainable practices. And...' She paused, gathering courage. 'And I love him,

Papai. I love him in a way I never thought possible.'

Miguel leaned back in his chair, his expression unreadable. 'Love is a beautiful thing, *minha filha*. But it's not always practical when it comes to running a farm that employs forty-three people and supports an entire community.'

'I know that,' Elena said, desperation creeping into her voice. 'But what if love and practicality don't have to be mutually exclusive? What if Guy's expertise could help us expand sustainably, create more employment, and support the community even better than before?'

'Elena,' her father's voice was gentle but firm, 'you're asking me to entrust our family's legacy to a stranger. A man I've never met, who has no experience with coffee cultivation, who doesn't speak our language or understand our culture.'

Elena felt tears threaten, but forced herself to remain composed. 'He's not a stranger to me, *Papai*. And yes, he'll need to learn about coffee, about our culture. But his fundamental approach to farming, his respect for the land—those can cross crops and continents.'

Miguel was quiet for a long moment, studying his daughter's face through the screen. When he spoke again, his voice carried a sadness Elena had never heard before.

'When I was your age,' he said slowly, 'I had dreams of studying architecture in Europe. Your grandfather's generation was traditional, resistant to change, and I thought I could leave.'

'What happened?' she asked softly.

'Your grandfather became ill,' Miguel replied. 'The farm needed management, the family needed support. I put aside my dreams and took over the operation. I don't regret that choice, Elena—it gave me your mother, you, and your brothers, a life I'm proud of. But I sometimes wonder what I might have achieved in my life, what opportunities I missed because my father was too focused on maintaining what already existed.'

Elena felt her heart skip. *'Papai...'*

'I won't let fear of change prevent my daughter from exploring possibilities I was too cautious to pursue,' Miguel continued. 'But Elena, I need to know this man understands what he's committing to. This isn't just about helping you implement new farming techniques—he'd be joining a family, a community, a way of life that may be very different from what he knows.'

Elena nodded eagerly. 'He understands that. Guy isn't looking for an adventure or a temporary change of scenery. He's looking for a life, a place where he can contribute meaningfully while building something lasting.'

'And if it doesn't work?' Miguel asked pragmatically. 'If the reality proves more difficult than the fantasy?'

'Then we adapt,' Elena replied, borrowing Guy's quiet confidence. 'We learn from our mistakes and find solutions. But *Papai*, what if it does work? What if bringing Guy into our operation is exactly what we need to take the farm to the next level?'

Miguel smiled for the first time since the conversation had turned serious. 'You sound like your grandmother when she convinced your grandfather to modernise the processing facility in 1987. Everyone thought she was crazy, but it tripled our productivity within two seasons.'

'So, you'll consider it?' Elena hardly dared

to hope.

'I'll do more than consider it,' Miguel replied. 'I want to meet this Guy Johnson. Can you arrange a video call? Tomorrow, perhaps?'

Elena felt relief flood through her so powerfully she nearly cried. 'Yes, of course. Any time that works for you.'

'Excellent. And Elena?' Her father's expression grew serious again. 'I'm proud of you for pursuing what you believe in, even when it complicates everything we've planned. That takes courage—the same courage your great-great-grandmother showed when she convinced her husband to purchase our first coffee plants.'

After the call ended, Elena sat in her cabin for several minutes, overwhelmed by the mixture of relief, excitement, and lingering anxiety that coursed through her. Her father was willing to meet Guy to consider the possibility of bringing an Australian farmer into their Brazilian operation. It wasn't approval yet, but it was hope.

She found Guy in the equipment shed, methodically cleaning and organising tools with the kind of focused attention he usually reserved for complex agricultural problems. When he looked up and saw her expression, his entire posture changed.

'How did it go?' he asked quietly.

'He wants to meet you,' Elena replied, unable to suppress the smile that spread across her face. 'Tomorrow afternoon, video call. He's... he's open to the possibility, Guy. Cautious, but open.'

Guy set down the wrench he'd been holding and crossed to her in three quick strides, sweeping her into his arms with a joy that made Elena laugh despite her emotional state.

'Thank you,' he whispered against her hair. 'Thank you for taking this chance, for believing it could work.'

Elena pulled back to look at his face, seeing hope and determination mingled with a vulnerability that made her heart ache with love. 'I should be thanking you,' she replied. 'For offering to turn your entire life upside down for someone you've known for a very short time.'

'Sometimes,' Guy said, his voice soft but certain, 'a day is enough to know everything that matters.'

Chapter 9

The Johnson family kitchen had been transformed into an impromptu conference room, with Elena's laptop positioned at the head of the table and chairs arranged to accommodate what Amelia had dramatically termed "the most important business meeting in farm history". The video call with Miguel Santiago was scheduled for two o'clock, and by one-thirty, the entire family had found reasons to hover nearby.

'You don't all need to be here,' Guy said for the third time, adjusting his tie with nervous fingers. He'd chosen his best shirt and jacket, the same ones he'd worn to Charlotte's engagement dinner, and Elena had to admit he looked impressive—professional but approachable, every inch the capable farmer he was.

'Of course we need to be here,' Amelia declared, fussing with the flowers she'd arranged as a backdrop. 'This is a momentous occasion. Elena's father needs to see that Guy comes from good stock.'

'He's not buying cattle, Amelia,' Oliver

observed dryly, though he made no move to leave the kitchen.

Elena checked the connection one more time, her stomach churning with nervous energy. So much depended on the next hour—not just her relationship with Guy, but the future she'd been afraid to envision, the possibility of choosing love without abandoning duty.

'He's going to love you,' she told Guy quietly, taking his hand under the table. 'My father respects competence and innovation above everything else. Once he sees your knowledge and your commitment...'

'What if he asks questions I can't answer?' Guy interrupted, voicing the fear that had been plaguing him since agreeing to this meeting. 'I know about sustainable agriculture, but coffee cultivation specifically... it feels like a job interview, and I've never even had one of them.'

'Is something you can learn,' Elena finished firmly. '*Papai* isn't expecting you to be a coffee expert—he's expecting you to be an expert in farming. And you are.'

As the laptop chimed with an incoming call, Guy's grandparents burst through the door.

'Are we too late?' *Grandmère* asked.

'Shh,' Amelia hissed. 'Come and stand over here.'

Guy's nerves fled as he looked up and saw his family all standing together across the table. Somehow, even Julien had got wind of what was happening and was standing next to Oliver. Guy shook his head. 'I don't believe you lot.'

'Ready?' Elana grinned up at him. 'Have I told you I love your family?'

He nodded, squeezing her hand once before releasing it and straightening in his chair. *Grandmère* and Papa walked across to stand behind Guy. 'I wish to meet your father,' *Grandmère* said to Elena.

Miguel Santiago's face appeared on the screen, his expression serious but not unwelcoming. Elena had briefed him on the family dynamic, so he didn't seem surprised to see additional faces behind Guy and Elena.

'*Papai*,' Elena said warmly, 'I'd like you to meet Guy Johnson and his family. Guy, this is my father, Miguel Santiago.'

'Mr Santiago,' Guy said, his voice steady despite the tension Elena could see in his shoulders. 'It's an honour to meet you. Elena speaks of you and your farm with tremendous respect.'

Miguel's expression softened slightly at the formal address. 'And she speaks of you with great enthusiasm, Mr Johnson. Both your agricultural expertise and your... personal qualities.'

Elena felt heat rise in her cheeks, but Guy's composure never wavered. 'Elena is an exceptional woman, sir. Her knowledge and passion for sustainable farming have taught me a great deal.'

'So I understand,' Miguel replied. 'Elena tells me you're interested in bringing your expertise to our operation in Brazil. That's quite a significant undertaking for someone who has never worked with coffee cultivation.'

Guy leaned forward slightly, his manner respectful but confident. 'You're absolutely right, Mr Santiago. I have no experience with coffee specifically. But I do have fifteen years of experience with sustainable agriculture, water management, and soil conservation. I've worked with crops that require careful climate control, precise nutrient management, and sustainable harvesting practices.'

'Coffee is not sugar cane, Mr Johnson.'

'No, sir, it's not,' Guy agreed readily. 'But the fundamental principles of working with the land, of creating systems that support both productivity and environmental sustainability—those principles apply regardless of the specific crop.'

Miguel nodded thoughtfully. 'Elena mentioned your water management systems. Can you tell me more about these techniques?'

What followed was a detailed technical discussion that gradually drew in other members of the Johnson family. Hugo joined his parents behind Guy and contributed insights about implementing new systems on established farms, while Oliver shared experiences with crop diversification. Elena watched her father's expression shift from polite attention to genuine interest as Guy demonstrated both his expertise and his ability to adapt that knowledge to different agricultural contexts.

'Your approach is systematic,' Miguel observed after Guy had explained his drainage innovations. 'Methodical, but creative. These are good qualities for agriculture.'

'Thank you, sir,' Guy replied. 'I learned from my father that lasting improvements come from understanding what already works before attempting to change what doesn't.'

Miguel's smile was the first genuinely warm expression Elena had seen from him during the call. 'Your father sounds like a wise man.'

'He is,' his father interjected from behind Guy's shoulder. 'And if I may say so, Mr Santiago, Guy is our most innovative son. His willingness to consider new approaches has kept our farm competitive in challenging markets.'

'Yet you're willing to let him go?' Miguel asked shrewdly.

Hugo's expression grew serious. 'I'm willing to let him choose his own path. Guy has given our family farm fifteen years of dedicated service. If his path now leads to Brazil, he goes with our support and blessing.'

Elena felt tears prick her eyes at the quiet pride in Hugo's voice. The Johnson family was demonstrating exactly the kind of support and understanding she hoped her own father would offer.

Miguel leaned back in his chair, studying Guy's face through the screen. 'Mr Johnson, Elena has told me about your feelings for my daughter. But feelings are not always sufficient for the practical realities of running a farm. What would you do if the technical challenges proved more difficult than anticipated? If the cultural adjustment was harder than expected?'

Guy didn't hesitate. 'I'd learn, sir. I'd ask questions, study the challenges, and adapt my approach until I found solutions that worked. That's what farming is—constant learning, constant adaptation.'

'And if your relationship with Elena became strained under the pressure of working together and living in a foreign country?'

This time, Guy paused, and Elena could see him choosing his words carefully. 'Mr Santiago, I can't promise that challenges wouldn't arise. But I can promise that I'm committed to working through whatever difficulties we might encounter. Elena means too much to me to give up when things get complicated.'

Miguel was quiet for a long moment, and

Elena held her breath waiting for his verdict. When he finally spoke, his voice carried decisiveness.

'Mr Johnson, I find myself impressed by your knowledge, your approach to agriculture, and your obvious respect for my daughter. However, this is not a decision I can make alone. Our farm employs many people, supports families who have worked our land for generations. I need time to consider how best to integrate new expertise into our existing operation.'

Elena felt her heart sink, but Guy nodded understanding. 'Of course, sir. This is a significant decision for your entire operation.'

'However,' Miguel continued, and Elena's pulse quickened, 'I would like to extend an invitation. Elena is scheduled to return to Brazil in six weeks. I would like you to accompany her, Mr Johnson. A trial period—perhaps two months—where you can see our operation firsthand, learn about coffee cultivation, and demonstrate how your expertise might benefit our farm.'

Elena gasped, hardly daring to believe what

she was hearing. Guy's face transformed with a smile so brilliant it made her heart skip.

'I would be honoured to accept that invitation, Mr Santiago,' Guy said, his voice thick with emotion. 'Thank you for giving me—us—this opportunity.'

'Don't thank me yet,' Miguel replied with a smile of his own. 'Coffee farming is demanding work, and Brazil is very different from Australia. You may decide after two months that this experiment was a mistake.'

'Or he may decide it's exactly where he belongs,' Elena interjected, unable to contain her joy any longer.

'*Talvez*,' Miguel agreed. 'Perhaps indeed.'

After the call ended and the whole family sat around the table with a pot of tea, accompanied by congratulations and excited planning discussions, Elena and Guy stepped out onto the back porch, still processing what had just occurred.

'Two months,' Guy said, as if testing the reality of it. 'Two months in Brazil, learning coffee cultivation, proving I can adapt to your world.'

'Two months for you to fall in love with my country the way I've fallen in love with yours,' Elena replied, moving to stand in front of him. 'Guy, are you sure about this? Once we get to Brazil, once you meet my family and see the scope of the responsibility...'

Guy silenced her with a gentle kiss, his hands framing her face with infinite tenderness. 'Elena Santiago,' he said when they broke apart, 'I have never been more certain of anything in my life. Two months, two years, twenty years—wherever you are is where I want to be.'

Elena's tears spilled over as she kissed him again, thinking of a future she'd never dared to hope for.

Chapter 10

Six weeks later, Elena stood in the departure lounge of Brisbane Airport, her hand intertwined with Guy's as they watched planes taxi along the runway. Their luggage—a carefully packed collection of farming texts and personal belongings—was checked through to São Paulo, and in three hours they would board the flight that would carry them towards a future neither had dreamed of just months before.

The weeks had passed in a blur of preparation and farewell gatherings. Guy had worked with Oliver and Hugo to ensure the farm's smooth operation in his absence, while Elena had coordinated with her father to arrange temporary housing and introduce Guy to key personnel at the Santiago plantation. The drainage system installation had been completed ahead of schedule, providing a concrete legacy of their collaboration that would benefit the Johnson farm for years to come.

But it was the smaller moments Elena would remember most clearly: Guy patiently learning basic Portuguese phrases from a language app, her growing comfort with the Johnson family, who had all become very dear to her, the quiet conversations about dreams and fears that had deepened their connection every day.

'Second thoughts?' Elena asked softly, noting the way Guy's gaze lingered on the Australian landscape visible through the terminal windows.

'Not about you,' Guy replied immediately, squeezing her hand. 'About leaving my family, about the magnitude of what we're attempting— yes, there are moments of uncertainty. But about us, about this choice we're making together? Never.'

Elena smiled, leaning against his shoulder as they watched other travellers hurry past with their own journeys and destinations. 'My father called this morning,' she said. 'Final confirmation that housing is arranged, that the farm managers are prepared for your arrival. He sounded... excited, actually. I think he's looking forward to having someone new to teach.'

'I'm looking forward to learning,' Guy admitted. 'Your descriptions of the plantation, the processing facilities, the community your family has built—it sounds incredible.'

'It is incredible,' Elena agreed. 'But it's also challenging, demanding, sometimes overwhelming. There will be days when you question whether leaving Australia was a mistake.'

Guy turned to face her fully, his expression serious but untroubled. 'Elena, every choice involves risk. Staying safe, staying comfortable—that's not really living, it's just existing. What we're doing, this leap we're taking together, it might fail spectacularly. But it might also be the best decision either of us has ever made.'

Elena felt her heart swell with love for this man who had proven willing to risk everything familiar for the chance to build something extraordinary with her. 'Whatever happens in Brazil—'

'Whatever happens,' Guy interrupted gently, 'we'll face it together. That's what partnerships are about, right? Sharing both the challenges and the victories?'

Their flight was called, and as they gathered

their carry-on bags and joined the queue of passengers, Elena was so happy, it almost hurt. For three years, she'd travelled Australia learning techniques and gathering experience to take back to Brazil. But the most valuable thing she was bringing home wasn't knowledge about drainage systems or soil management—it was Guy himself, and the love that had taught her to see her responsibilities as opportunities.

As their plane lifted off from Brisbane, carrying them towards Brazil, Elena looked out the window at the Queensland countryside growing smaller below them.

'I'll miss your family,' she said quietly.

'They'll be there when we visit, and we've got three weddings coming up in the next year,' Guy reminded her. 'Plus, Oliver's already planning a trip to Brazil for next year, and Amelia's started learning Portuguese. You haven't lost the Johnson family, Elena—you've just expanded yours.'

Elena smiled at the thought of Amelia attempting to navigate Brazilian culture with her usual dramatic flair, of Oliver and Sarah bringing Jett to explore the coffee plantation, of the two families that had shaped her and Guy coming together across continents and cultures.

'What are you thinking about?' Guy asked, noting her expression.

'The future,' Elena replied. 'All the things I hadn't even thought about six months ago.'

Guy nodded, his own gaze turning towards the window. 'Whatever the next two months bring, whatever challenges we discover, whatever adjustments we need to make—this feels right, Elena. Choosing love, choosing each other, choosing to chase our dreams.'

Chapter 11

Two months later

Elena stood on the terraced hillside that overlooked her family's coffee plantation, watching Guy demonstrate proper pruning techniques to a group of workers who had gathered to learn from the Australian farmer who had surprised everyone with his quick adaptation to Brazilian agriculture. The morning sun cast long shadows across the rows of glossy-leafed plants, and the air was sweet with the scent of coffee blossoms and rich earth.

Guy's Portuguese had improved dramatically, aided by total immersion and his natural ear for languages. More importantly, his agricultural innovations had begun to show measurable results—improved water efficiency, healthier soil conditions, and early indicators of increased yield that had impressed even the most traditional workers on the plantation.

But it wasn't the technical success that made Elena's heart swell with happiness as she watched him work. It was the easy way he'd integrated into the community, his genuine respect for the knowledge of workers who had been cultivating coffee for decades, his obvious joy in learning new approaches to the agricultural work he loved.

'He fits,' her father's voice came from beside her, and Elena turned to see Miguel approaching with his morning coffee and the satisfied expression he wore when reviewing particularly successful crop reports.

'He does,' Elena agreed, accepting the second cup he offered her. 'Better than either of us dared hope.'

'Your mother adores him,' Miguel continued with a smile. 'She says he reminds her of her own father—quiet strength, genuine kindness, complete dedication to the land. And to you, my dear.'

Elena laughed softly. 'Guy's still adjusting to the level of family involvement in Brazilian culture. Australian families are close, but Brazilian families are...'

'Inescapable,' Miguel finished with a grin. 'But he seems to appreciate it, even when your aunts interrogate him about wedding plans.'

Elena's cheeks warmed. The marriage

question had become a frequent topic of family discussion, though she and Guy had been focused on establishing their working partnership before addressing their personal commitment.

'Speaking of which,' Miguel said casually, 'I had an interesting conversation with your young man yesterday. About long-term plans, about his intentions regarding both you and the plantation.'

Elena's pulse quickened. 'What kind of conversation?'

'The kind a father has with a man who wants to marry his daughter and become a permanent partner in the family business,' Miguel replied, his eyes twinkling with amusement at Elena's expression. 'He asked for my blessing, Elena. Both personal and professional.'

Elena nearly dropped her coffee cup. 'He did?'

'Quite formally, quite respectfully. I was impressed by his seriousness, his clear understanding of what he's committing to.' Miguel paused, studying his daughter's face. 'I gave him both, of course. How could I refuse a man who has already proven his dedication to our family and our farm?'

Elena's tears spilled over as she looked back towards Guy, who had noticed their observation and was walking towards them with that easy smile that never failed to make her heart skip. In his hands, he carried a small cutting from one of the coffee plants—probably another sample for the soil analysis project they'd been working on together.

'Good morning, Miguel,' Guy said as he approached, his Portuguese now fluent enough for comfortable conversation. 'The workers are eager to try the new pruning method on the eastern slopes. José thinks we could see a fifteen percent increase in yield next season.'

'Excellent news,' Miguel replied, though his eyes held a knowing gleam that made Elena's pulse quicken. 'Guy, I was just telling Elena about our conversation yesterday.'

Guy's expression shifted subtly, and Elena caught the flicker of nervousness that crossed his features before being replaced by determination. 'Ah,' he said simply, his gaze moving to Elena's face. 'I hope you don't mind that I spoke to your father first. It seemed... appropriate, given the cultural context.'

Elena felt her heart begin to race as understanding dawned. 'Guy...'

'Elena Santiago,' Guy said, his voice soft but steady as he reached into his pocket and withdrew a small velvet box. 'I know we've built our relationship on practical partnerships and shared agricultural goals. But somewhere between drainage systems and coffee cultivation, I discovered that what I really want is to spend the rest of my life learning new things with you.'

Elena's breath caught as Guy dropped to one knee on the hillside overlooking the plantation that represented five generations of her family's work—the place where she'd finally learned to choose both love and duty, both personal happiness and family responsibility.

'Will you marry me?' he asked, opening the box to reveal a ring that somehow perfectly captured the golden warmth of coffee blossoms and Queensland sunlight combined. 'Will you let me be your partner in all things—farming and family, dreams and daily life, whatever adventures we discover together?'

Elena looked down at this man who had proven willing to transform his entire existence for love, who had embraced her world with the same quiet dedication he'd shown his own, who had taught her that the most meaningful choices weren't between duty and desire but about finding ways to honour both.

'Yes,' she whispered, then louder, with all the joy and certainty she felt flooding through her: 'Yes, Guy Johnson. Yes, to everything.'

As Guy slipped the ring onto her finger and rose to kiss her, Elena heard her father's delighted laughter mixing with the distant voices of workers who had paused in their tasks to witness the proposal. Somewhere across the world, she knew, the Johnson family was probably just sitting down to breakfast, unaware that their quiet son had just taken the final step in claiming a Brazilian future.

But they would know soon enough. And in a few months, when the families gathered for what Amelia would undoubtedly orchestrate as the wedding of the century, the terraced hills of the Santiago plantation would echo with Australian accents and Portuguese celebration, two agricultural legacies joining to create something entirely new.

For now, though, it was enough to stand in Guy's arms on the land that had shaped her entire life, watching the morning sun paint the coffee plants in shades of gold and promise, knowing that sometimes the most impossible dreams turned out to be the most inevitable truths.

The coffee harvest was just beginning, and Elena Santiago—soon to be Elena Johnson, or perhaps Elena Santiago-Johnson, depending on how they negotiated that particular cultural bridge—had never been more ready for the work ahead.

Chapter 12

Two weeks after their engagement, Guy stood in the pre-dawn darkness of the coffee plantation, watching the mist rise from the terraced hillsides like something from a dream. The air was sweet with the scent of coffee blossoms and rich earth, and despite the early hour, he could already hear the distant voices of workers beginning their day in the processing facility below.

His Portuguese had improved dramatically through total immersion, and his understanding of coffee cultivation had grown from theoretical knowledge to practical expertise under Miguel Santiago's patient tutelage. The water management systems he'd proposed were showing early signs of success, and even the most traditional workers had begun to seek his opinion on soil conditions and sustainable practices.

But this morning, as Guy checked his phone for messages from home, a familiar ache of homesickness settled in his chest. It had been three weeks since he'd spoken to his family beyond brief text updates, the time difference and busy harvest season making longer conversations difficult to coordinate.

Elena emerged from the plantation house carrying two steaming cups of coffee, her hair pulled back in the practical braid she favoured for field work. Even in simple work clothes, she took Guy's breath away—not just her beauty, but the confidence with which she moved through her family's land, the easy authority she'd assumed in managing the expansion project that had become their shared focus.

'You're up early,' she observed, settling beside him on the stone wall that bordered the main terrace. 'Couldn't sleep?'

'I keep thinking about our farm at home,' Guy admitted, accepting the coffee gratefully. 'Whether they've started the mango harvest, how the new irrigation system is performing, whether Dad's remembering to take his heart medication regularly.'

Elena's expression softened with understanding. 'You miss them.'

'I do,' Guy said simply. 'More than I

expected, if I'm honest. Not enough to regret this choice' —he gestured towards the spectacular view of the plantation, towards Elena herself— 'but enough to make me appreciate how difficult this transition has been.'

'Have you talked to your father recently? About how he's managing without you?'

Guy shook his head. 'We text occasionally, but he's never been one for long phone conversations. And I don't want him to think I'm doubting my decision by calling too often.'

Elena studied his face in the growing light, noting the tension around his eyes that had been building over the past week. 'Guy, your father had a heart attack less than two years ago. It's natural to worry about his health, especially when you're so far away.'

Before Guy could respond, his phone buzzed with an incoming call. Oliver's name appeared on the screen, and Guy felt his stomach tighten with instant anxiety. His brother rarely called, preferring texts for routine communication. A phone call at this hour suggested something urgent.

'Oliver?' Guy answered immediately,

switching to speaker so Elena could hear.

'Guy, mate, I'm glad I caught you.' Oliver's voice carried a strain that made Guy's pulse quicken. 'Dad's had another heart attack.'

The world seemed to tilt around Guy, the peaceful morning suddenly feeling surreal and distant. 'How bad?'

'He's stable now, in hospital in Bundaberg. But Guy... the doctors are saying it was more severe than last time. They're talking about surgery, possibly another bypass operation. The prognosis is...' Oliver's voice cracked slightly. 'They're not sure how much more strain his heart can take.'

Elena reached for Guy's free hand, her grip steady and warm as he struggled to process what he was hearing.

'I'm coming home,' Guy said immediately, his mind already racing through flight schedules and packing requirements. 'I can probably get a flight out tomorrow, maybe tonight if—'

'Guy, wait,' Oliver interrupted gently. 'Before you make any decisions, you should know—Dad specifically asked me to tell you not to rush back. He said, and I quote, "That boy finally found his path. I won't have him derailing his future because of my dicky heart.'"

Tears pricked Guy's eyes. Even facing serious health issues, his father was more concerned about his son's happiness than his own well-being.

'That's exactly why I need to come home,' Guy replied, his voice thick with emotion. 'Oliver, if something happens to Dad and I'm not there...'

'I understand,' Oliver said quietly. 'And if you decide to come home, we'll all support that choice.'

Elena squeezed Guy's hand, drawing his attention to her face. Her expression held a mixture of compassion and determination that he'd come to recognise when she was working through complex problems.

'What do the doctors say about the timeline?' she asked, leaning closer to the phone. 'For surgery, for recovery?'

'The surgery is scheduled for next week,' Oliver replied. 'Recovery could be several months, depending on how well it goes. The doctors are being cautious, but...' He paused, clearly struggling with his own emotions. 'It's serious, Elena. More serious than any of us wants to admit.'

Guy stared out across the coffee plantation, his mind torn between the life he'd been building in Brazil and the family crisis unfolding thousands of miles away. How could he stay here, learning about coffee cultivation and planning his future with Elena, while his father faced life-threatening surgery alone?

'I have to go back,' he said finally. 'At least for the surgery, to be there for Mum and the family. Elena, I'm sorry, but—'

'Of course you have to go back,' Elena interrupted, her voice firm with conviction. 'Your father needs you, your family needs you. We'll figure out the rest later.'

'We?' Guy looked at her questioningly.

Elena smiled, though he could see the worry in her eyes. 'Did you think I'd let you face this alone? Guy, if your father is having surgery, if your family is in crisis, then my place is beside you. My work here can wait.'

'Elena, you can't leave now,' Guy protested. 'The expansion project is at a critical stage, your father needs you to oversee the implementation—'

'My father managed this plantation for forty years before I returned from Australia,' Elena reminded him gently. 'He can manage it for a few more weeks while I support the man I love through a family emergency.'

Guy felt his heart constrict with gratitude and love for this woman who was willing to put her own responsibilities aside to be with him during the crisis.

'Are you sure?' he asked. 'Elena, this could change everything. If Dad's recovery is complicated, if he needs long-term care—'

'Then we'll adapt,' Elena said simply. 'Guy, when I agreed to build a life with you, I didn't sign up only for the easy parts. Family emergencies, health crises, unexpected challenges—that's all part of loving someone completely.'

Oliver's voice came through the phone, gentle but urgent. 'Whatever you both decide, you should know that flights to Australia are booked solid for the next three days. I've already checked. The earliest I could get you on a plane would be Thursday.'

Guy felt panic rise in his chest. 'Thursday? That's four days away. What if—'

'What if nothing,' Elena said firmly, standing and pulling Guy to his feet. 'We'll get to Australia as soon as humanly possible. In the meantime, your father is receiving excellent medical care, and he's surrounded by people who love him. That's going to have to be enough.'

As they walked back towards the plantation house to begin the urgent process of arranging travel and adjusting work schedules, Guy closed his eyes, shocked by how dramatically his life could change in the space of a single phone call. Two months ago, he'd been concerned about adapting to coffee cultivation and Brazilian culture. Now he faced the possibility of losing his father and having to choose between the new life he'd built with Elena and the family responsibilities waiting for him in Australia.

But as Elena's hand found his, steady and sure in the growing daylight, Guy realised that love meant facing life's challenges together— not choosing between them, but finding ways to work together.

The coffee plants would still be growing when they returned. The question was whether they would be returning together, and whether the life they'd begun to build in Brazil could survive the test of an Australian family crisis.

***

The São Paulo airport was a chaos of travellers, announcements in multiple languages, and the barely controlled urgency that characterised international terminals during peak tourist season. Elena sat beside Guy in the departure lounge, watching him stare at his phone with the kind of intensity that suggested he was willing messages from home to appear through sheer determination.

It had taken three frantic days to arrange their travel, with Elena's father personally making calls to contacts in the airline industry to secure seats on a flight that was booked out months in advance. Miguel had been unquestioningly supportive of their decision to return to Australia, handling the plantation's immediate needs and assuring Elena that her place was with Guy during his family crisis.

'The last update from Amelia was four hours ago,' Guy said, refreshing his messages for the dozenth time. 'Dad was stable, asking about the farm, apparently giving the nurses grief about hospital food.'

'That sounds promising,' Elena replied, though she could see the strain in Guy's expression. 'Your father's too stubborn to let a heart attack defeat him easily.'

Guy managed a weak smile. 'That's what I keep telling myself. But Elena, what if we're too late? What if something happens during the flight and I never get to—'

'Stop,' Elena interrupted gently, taking his phone and setting it aside. 'You can't control timing or outcomes or any of the things that terrify you right now. All you can control is being there for your family when they need you.'

Guy nodded, though his leg continued bouncing with nervous energy. 'I keep thinking about the last conversation I had with Dad before we left Australia. I was so focused on explaining why Brazil was the right choice, so determined to convince him I wasn't abandoning the family. I should have told him how much he means to me, how grateful I am for everything he taught me about farming and responsibility and how to be a good man.'

Elena's heart ached for the regret in Guy's voice. 'He knows all of that already, Guy. Fathers don't need grand declarations to understand how their sons feel about them.'

'Don't they?' Guy looked at her with an expression that was almost childlike in its need for reassurance. 'Elena, what if I've made a terrible mistake? What if coming to Brazil was selfish? What if Dad needed me here and I was too caught up in my own happiness to see it?'

Elena turned to face him fully, her expression serious but compassionate. 'Guy Johnson, listen to me carefully. Your father had a heart attack because he has a medical condition, not because you fell in love and moved to South America. You did not cause this crisis, and you are not responsible for preventing it.'

'But if I'd been there—'

'If you'd been there, you would have worried constantly about his health instead of living your own life,' Elena interrupted. 'And that's not what your father wanted for you. The man who raised you to be thoughtful and responsible and capable of love—that man wanted you to be happy. Don't dishonour his parenting by turning your happiness into a source of guilt.'

Guy stared at her for a long moment, then pulled her into his arms with sudden fierce intensity. 'I love you so much,' he whispered against her hair. 'I love you for coming with me, for understanding why I need to be there, for not making me choose between you and my family.'

'You're not choosing,' Elena reminded him. 'We're facing this together, whatever comes next.'

Their flight was called, and as they joined the queue of passengers heading towards the gate, Elena refused to let uncertainty take hold. They were flying towards a medical crisis that could fundamentally alter their lives, towards a family that would be grappling potentially devastating loss.

But they were together, united by love. Whatever they found when they reached Australia, whatever decisions needed to be made about the future, they would make them together.

139

Chapter 13

The hospital waiting room had that particular smell of disinfectant and anxiety that seemed to seep into everything. Ellen sat rigid in the plastic chair, her knuckles white as she gripped Guy's hand. Across from them, other members of the family tried to make conversation, but their words felt hollow in the sterile space.

Hugo had been in surgery for nearly six hours now. What had started as a routine procedure had stretched on, each passing hour adding weight to the silence between them.

Guy squeezed his mother's hand. 'He's strong, Mum,' he murmured, though his own voice betrayed his worry. 'Dad's the strongest man I know.'

Ellen nodded, but her eyes remained fixed on the double doors marked 'Authorised Personnel Only' – the same doors through which the surgeon had disappeared what felt like a lifetime ago. 'He hasn't been following the diet he was supposed to stay on, and he often forgets his medication. It's my fault. I should have made sure he did.'

When those doors finally swung open, Dr. Webb emerged, still in his surgical scrubs. His expression was carefully neutral, but something in his posture made Guy tense. Ellen jumped up from her chair, and Guy was immediately beside her, his arm around her waist.

'Mrs. Johnson.' Dr. Webb's voice was gentle but tired.

'Yes,' Ellen managed, her voice barely above a whisper. 'How is he? Is he...?

'Your husband is alive, Mrs. Johnson. The surgery was successful in that regard.' Dr. Webb paused, choosing his words carefully. 'However, we did encounter some complications that I need to discuss with you.'

Guy caught his mother as her legs gave way, pulling her tight against his chest. His heart was hammering so hard he was sure she could feel it through his shirt. This couldn't be happening. Not now. Not to his father.

'Let's sit down,' Dr. Webb said kindly, gesturing to the chairs. Guy helped his mother back into her seat, not letting go of her hand.

'What kind of complications?' he asked, his voice steady despite the fear coursing through him.

Dr. Webb pulled up a chair to face them directly. 'During the procedure, your father suffered what we call a cardiac event; his heart stopped briefly. We were able to resuscitate him, but he was without oxygen for several minutes. Additionally, there was more damage to his heart than our initial scans had shown.'

Guy felt the room closing in around him. Ellen was trembling against his side, and he tightened his grip on her.

'What does that mean?' she asked.

'It means recovery will be a long process, Mrs. Johnson. A very long process. Your husband will live, but...' Dr. Webb's pause seemed to stretch forever. 'He may never regain full mobility. The cardiac event means he'll need extensive rehabilitation. Even then, there's no guarantee he'll return to his previous level of physical capability.'

The silence that followed was deafening.

'Can we see him?' Guy asked quietly.

'He's being moved to intensive care. He's

sedated now, but you can see him briefly. I should warn you—he's on a ventilator, and there are a lot of machines. It can be overwhelming.'

Ellen nodded, though she wasn't sure she was ready for any of this.

***

Three hours later, after they'd taken turns sitting beside Hugo's bed, watching the steady rise and fall of the ventilator, the family gathered around the old oak table in the kitchen at the farmhouse. Guy looked around at the faces assembled there; each of his siblings who lived locally was there, and Lisette was on her way home.

Grandmère sat hunched in her chair, looking as though she had aged a decade in the space of a single day. The strong, spirited woman who had always been the backbone of their family seemed fragile suddenly, her wrinkled hands shaking as she clutched a cup of tea that had long gone cold. Papa sat close beside her, his own lined hand covering hers in a gesture of quiet comfort. Guy had never seen his grandfather look so helpless.

Ellen sat at Hugo's usual place at the head of

the table, though she looked anything but in charge. Her eyes were red from crying, and she kept wringing her hands in her lap. Guy took his usual seat to her right.

'We need to talk about what happens now,' Guy said gently, breaking the heavy silence. The words felt strange in his mouth – he was supposed to be the one leaving, not the one making plans for staying.

'Dad is going to get better,' Amelia said firmly. 'The doctor said he'll live.'

'Yes, but...' Ellen's voice cracked. 'He said your father might never... might never be able to work the farm again.'

Guy watched *Grandmère*'s face crumple at those words. Seeing her son lying motionless in that hospital bed seemed to have broken something in her.

'We'll manage,' Guy heard himself say, though the words felt like they were coming from someone else. 'Between all of us, we can keep things running until Dad's back on his feet.'

'But what if he's never back on his feet?' Ellen asked, voicing the question that Guy had been trying not to think about. 'What if this is it?

What if he can't... what if he needs care for the rest of his life?'

Guy looked around the table, seeing his fears reflected in every face. His father—the strongest man he knew – might never walk properly again. Might never be able to run the farm. Might need full-time care.

Grandmère made a small, broken sound, and Robert's arm tightened around her shoulders. '*Mon fils*,' she whispered. 'My son.'

'Then we'll take care of him,' Oliver said firmly. 'Just like he's always taken care of us.'

Chapter 14

The kettle whistled softly as Guy prepared his father's evening tea, adding just a splash of milk the way Hugo liked it. Three months had passed since the surgery, and while Hugo was home and slowly recovering, the weight of unspoken decisions hung heavy in the farmhouse air. Through the kitchen window, Guy could see his father's silhouette on the front porch, wrapped in a blanket despite the warm evening, watching the sun paint the sky in shades of gold and crimson.

It had been a difficult conversation earlier that day when Hugo had finally said the words they'd all been dreading. 'I won't be coming back to full work on the farm,' he'd told Guy and Oliver, his voice steady but his eyes betraying the grief of letting go. 'It's time for you boys to take over properly. I'm retiring.'

The announcement had settled the immediate question of the farm's future – Oliver and Guy would manage it together, combining Oliver's practical experience with Guy's business acumen. But it had done nothing to resolve the larger dilemma that kept Guy awake at night. Elena was here with him, but her family needed her back in Brazil. They were engaged, their futures supposedly intertwined, yet pulled in opposite directions by family obligations.

Guy picked up the steaming mug and headed for the door, his mind churning over solutions that all seemed to lead to heartbreak. Either Elena would have to return to Brazil alone, or he would have to abandon his recovering father and the farm that now depended on him. There seemed to be no path forward that didn't require sacrificing something precious.

The screen door was about to swing shut behind him when he heard the sound of running footsteps on the gravel drive. Elena burst through the kitchen door, her face flushed with excitement and something that looked remarkably like joy.

'Guy!' she called out, slightly breathless from her run. 'Oh, Guy, I have news!'

He turned back, still holding the tea, struck by the contrast between her obvious excitement and his mood. 'What is it?'

'My father is going to retire too!' The words

tumbled out of her in a rush. 'He rang – he's been thinking about it since we left.'

Guy felt his face fall, the implications hitting him like a physical blow. If Elena's father was retiring, that meant the family would need Elena back in Brazil more than ever. Someone would have to take over the coffee plantation, and as the eldest daughter with the best head for business, that someone would undoubtedly be Elena. The mug trembled slightly in his hands.

'That's... that would be dreadful,' he said quietly, the words slipping out before he could stop them. 'It means you'll have to go home.'

Elena saw the devastation written across his features and stepped forward quickly, her hands reaching for his arms. 'No, Guy, no. You don't understand! Listen!'

'I understand perfectly,' he said, his voice hollow. 'Your family needs you. The plantation needs someone to run it, and you're the obvious choice. You'll have to go back.'

'Guy, listen to me!' Elena's grip tightened on his arms, her eyes bright with something that wasn't sadness. 'My father is selling the farm!'

The words didn't register at first. Guy stared

at her, certain he'd misheard. 'What?'

'He is selling the coffee plantation,' Elena repeated, her excitement bubbling over now that she had his attention. 'He's been thinking about it since we left. He's tired, Guy. He's found a buyer—a large agricultural company that's been after the land for years.'

Guy set the tea down on the kitchen counter with shaking hands. 'But... but your family. Your inheritance. Everything your father built...'

'Will provide very well for all of us,' Elena said, her smile growing wider. 'Papa says the sale will be enough to secure a comfortable retirement for him and Mama, and substantial settlements for me and my brothers. Enough that we can chase our own dreams instead of being tied to the plantation.'

'Chase your own dreams,' Guy repeated slowly, afraid to believe what he was hearing.

Elena nodded, her hands sliding up to cup his face. 'We can stay here, Guy. We can stay and help your family with this farm. We can build our life here, together, without having to choose between your family's needs and mine.'

The relief that washed over Guy was so

intense it left his head spinning. For months, he'd been preparing himself for the final goodbye, for watching Elena board a plane back to Brazil while he remained tied to the family land. The idea that they might not have to choose, that they could have both their love and their family obligations, seemed too good to be true.

'Are you sure?' he asked, his voice husky with emotion. 'Are you sure this is what you want? Queensland isn't São Paulo. The farm isn't the coffee plantation. It's a different life entirely.'

Elena's smile was radiant. 'I'm sure. I love it here, Guy. I love your family, I love the land, I love the work. And most of all, I love you. I want to build our life here, with your parents, and *Grandmère* and Papa, and Charlotte, and Julien, and Oliver and Amelia. I want to meet Lisette. I want to be part of this.'

Guy pulled her into his arms, holding her tight against his chest as the months of worry finally lifted. Through the kitchen window, he could see Dad still sitting on the porch, patient in his blanket, waiting for his tea and watching the last of the sunset fade into twilight.

'I should take Dad's tea out,' Guy said reluctantly, not wanting to let Elena go.

'Take it to him,' Elena agreed, but she caught his hand as he reached for the mug. 'And Guy? We should tell him the news. About Papa's decision, about us staying. I think it might make him happy to know that his retirement doesn't mean losing you after all.'

Guy nodded, understanding flooding through him. His father's greatest fear hadn't been about his own failing health; it had been about the burden his condition would place on his children, the choices they would be forced to make. Knowing that Guy could stay, that the farm would remain in family hands, that love hadn't been sacrificed for duty, that would indeed make Hugo very happy.

Hand in hand, they walked out to the porch together, Guy carrying the tea and Elena carrying the news that would change everything. The future, which had seemed so impossible just minutes before, now stretched out ahead of them full of promise and possibility.

Hugo looked up as they approached, his weathered face creasing into a smile at the sight of them together. 'You two look like you've got something to tell me,' he observed, accepting the tea with a grateful smile.

'We do, Hugo,' Elena said, settling into the chair beside him while Guy perched on the porch railing. 'We have some very good news.'

As Elena began to share the story of her father's decision, Guy watched the worry lines around his father's eyes begin to ease. Happiness filled him as he walked over and put his arm around his father's shoulder.

'I'm home to stay, Dad.'

Chapter 15

The farmhouse kitchen had never seen so much chaos, and that was saying something considering it had survived decades of family gatherings. Amelia stood at the centre of it all like a conductor orchestrating beautiful mayhem, simultaneously directing the flower arrangements while tormenting her brothers.

'Oliver, you've got frosting in your beard,' she announced sweetly, not bothering to look up from the roses she was arranging. 'Very distinguished. Very "I raided the wedding cake at midnight".'

Oliver's hand flew to his face, finding the telltale evidence of his pre-dawn reconnaissance mission. 'How did you—'

'I have eyes everywhere, dear brother. Also, Sarah ratted you out.' Amelia grinned as Sarah, who with Jett's help, was tying white bows on chairs in the adjoining room, called out an unapologetic 'Sorry, love!'

Guy watched the familiar sibling warfare with amusement, his arm around Elena's waist as she observed her first full Johnson family gathering.

'Is it always like this?' Elena ducked as Julien launched a tea towel at Amelia's head.

'This is actually quite tame,' Guy replied. 'Wait until after dinner when the stories start.'

Across the kitchen, Lisette was unpacking boxes of wine glasses, looking more relaxed than Guy had seen her in years. Her time at the art gallery had clearly agreed with her; there was a lightness in her step and a genuine smile that reached her eyes. When she'd walked into the farmhouse yesterday afternoon, Dad had actually teared up.

'Lisette,' Elena had said warmly when they'd been introduced, 'Guy's told me so much about you. I'm so glad you're home for the wedding.'

'Weddings,' Lisette had corrected with a laugh. 'Trust our family to complicate even the simple things.'

That revelation had come out over dinner two nights ago, when Charlotte and Greg had casually mentioned that Julien and Emily had decided they wanted a large wedding after all, and wouldn't it be lovely to have a double ceremony? The way Charlotte had said it, with barely concealed delight, made it clear this had been planned for weeks.

'You knew!' Amelia had accused, pointing her fork at Charlotte. 'You all knew and nobody told me!'

'We wanted it to be a surprise,' Emily had said, grinning. 'Besides, you would have tried to reorganise everything.'

'I would have *improved* everything,' Amelia had corrected with dignity.

Now, on the morning of the double wedding, the farmhouse hummed with barely controlled energy. Hugo sat at his usual place at the kitchen table, looking remarkably well despite the walking stick propped beside his chair. The decision to retire to the coast had been a good one; Ellen had been right that staying at the farm would have been torture for him, watching others do the work he'd done for decades.

'Elena, love,' Hugo called out. 'Come sit with an old man for a moment. These children are giving me a headache.'

'We're giving you a headache?' Julien protested. 'Amelia's the one terrorising everyone!'

'I'm creating atmosphere,' Amelia said serenely. 'There's a difference.'

Elena settled into the chair beside Hugo, accepting the cup of tea he poured. Guy watched his father's face soften as he looked at his soon-to-be daughter-in-law. The engagement ring on Elena's finger caught the morning light— a simple solitaire that had belonged to Ellen's mother.

'Nervous?' Hugo asked Elena quietly.

'About what?' she replied, confused.

'About becoming a part of this family,' Hugo said, gesturing around the kitchen where his children continued their good-natured chaos.

Elena's laugh was warm and genuine. 'Hugo, I've never been more certain of anything in my life.'

***

By late afternoon, the farmhouse had been transformed. White chairs lined the lawn in neat rows, facing an archway that Oliver had built and Sarah had decorated with native flowers. The old oak tree provided natural shade, and fairy lights strung between the branches would provide a magical glow once the sun set.

Guy stood at the makeshift altar beside Julien, both of them in their best suits, watching as their guests took their seats. The informal nature of the ceremony meant the audience was an eclectic mix: neighbouring farmers in their Sunday best sat beside Elena's family, who had flown in from Brazil, while *Grandmère* held court in the front row, resplendent in a hat that probably violated several aviation regulations according to Amelia.

'Breathe,' Guy murmured to Julien and Greg. 'You both look like you're about to pass out.' Greg was standing as best man for both his brother and his brother-in-law-to-be

'I'm fine,' Julien replied, then immediately proved himself wrong by tugging at his collar. 'Aren't you nervous, Greg?'

'Terrified,' Greg admitted cheerfully. 'But in a good way.'

The music began— a simple acoustic guitar played by one of Charlotte's friends – and the procession started. Amelia led the way as bridesmaid for both brides, looking uncharacteristically elegant in a flowing royal blue dress that she'd somehow managed not to spill anything on. Her hair was a soft pale blue with silver glints, and even *Grandmère* had approved of this week's colour choice. Amelia's usual mischievous grin was replaced by genuine emotion as she took her place.

Emily appeared first, radiant in a simple white dress, her bouquet of wildflowers reflecting her practical nature. She winked at Julien as she walked down the aisle, making him laugh and visibly relax.

Then Charlotte emerged, and Guy heard the collective intake of breath from the assembled guests. Her dress was pure French, with delicate lace sleeves and a train that whispered against the grass. But it was her face that made the moment magical—pure joy, the kind that comes from knowing you're exactly where you're meant to be.

Greg's face was a picture of wonder as Charlotte approached, and Guy felt his own throat tighten with emotion. He glanced back to the second row where Elena was sitting with her family, tears streaming down her cheeks, and Guy smiled at her. Soon. Soon it would be their turn.

The ceremony itself was a blur of traditional vows and personal promises, of rings exchanged and kisses celebrated. Hugo's voice was strong when he stood to offer his blessing, his walking stick steady as he spoke of love, family, and the home they'd all built together.

'Marriage,' he concluded, 'isn't about finding the perfect person. It's about choosing to love an imperfect person perfectly, every single day. These four have already figured that out.'

The informal supper that followed was everything Ameilia had promised had hoped for – long tables set up under the stars, platters of Ellen's cooking, and wine flowing freely as the stories began. *Grandmère* regaled Elena's family with tales of family romance, while Ellen and Hugo sat close to each other, holding hands and smiling.

The speeches were heartfelt and funny, with just enough embarrassing childhood stories to keep everyone entertained. When it came time for the bouquet toss, both brides stood back-to-back, bouquets ready.

Elena, positioned strategically by Amelia,

somehow managed to catch both bouquets simultaneously, much to everyone's amazement and delight.

'That was rigged,' Guy said, pulling her close.

'Completely,' Elena agreed, not looking remotely sorry about it.

As the evening wound down and the last of the dishes were being cleared, Amelia tapped her wine glass for attention.

'Before everyone gets too sentimental and weepy,' she announced, 'I have an announcement. I'm moving out.'

The table fell silent.

'You and Elena can have the farmhouse,' she continued, grinning at Guy's shocked expression. 'Oliver and Sarah are in their new house, the newlyweds will want their privacy, and I don't want to be a third wheel.'

'You can live in the spare room at the store,' Julien offered immediately.

'No, thank you,' Amelia replied with a shudder. 'I've found a cute little rental in town. Close enough to interfere in all your lives, far enough away to have my own space. It's perfect.'

The table erupted in protests and questions, but Amelia held up her hand. 'It's decided. Besides, Guy and Elena are going to need somewhere to plan their own wedding, and I refuse to listen to months of 'Should we have roses or carnations?' discussions ever again.'

Elena laughed, her arm tightening around Guy's waist. 'We haven't even set a date yet!'

'You will,' Amelia said confidently. 'And when you do, I'll be ready with a bigger, better hat.'

As the evening wound down and the last guests departed, Guy led Elena out to the porch, looking up at the star-filled sky. The farmhouse behind them was quiet now, his family settling into their own homes and new lives away from the old farmhouse where they had all grown up.

'Happy?' Elena asked, her head on his shoulder.

'More than I ever thought possible,' Guy replied honestly. 'Your turn next.'

Elena tilted her face up to look at him, her eyes bright with love and promise. 'Our turn next,' she corrected softly.

Guy kissed her gently. Tomorrow would

bring new challenges, but tonight, everything was perfect.

'*Our* turn next,' he murmured against her lips.

Also by Annie Seaton

Daughters of the Darling
From Across the Sea
Over the River
By the Billabong
Beneath Still Waters

A Bec Whitfield Mystery
Bowen River
Shadows on the Shore
Storm Season

Duckinwilla Days
Coming Home
Secrets and Surprises
Wishes and Whispers
Chasing Dreams
New Beginnings

The Enchanted Village series
A Magic Christmas

Home to the Outback
Lucy
Angie
Jemima
Isabella

Porter Sisters Series
Kakadu Sunset
Daintree
Diamond Sky
Hidden Valley
Larapinta
Kakadu Dawn

Others
Whitsunday Dawn
Undara
Osprey Reef
East of Alice
One Summer in Tuscany
Four Seasons Short and Sweet
Follow the Sun
Ten Days in Paradise
Deadly Secrets
Adventures in Time
Silver Valley Witch
The Emerald Necklace
A Clever Christmas
Christmas with the Boss
Her Christmas Star
The Emerald Necklace

The Augathella Girls Series
Outback Roads

Outback Sky
Outback Escape
Outback Wind
Outback Dawn
Outback Moonlight
Outback Dust
Outback Hope
Boxed Sets
Augathella Girls 1-4
Augathella Girls 5-8

Augathella Short and Sweet Series
An Augathella Surprise
An Augathella Baby
An Augathella Spring
An Augathella Christmas
An Augathella Wedding
An Augathella Easter
An Augathella Masquerade Ball
Boxed Set
Augathella Short and Sweet 1-3
Augathella Short and Sweet 1-4

Sunshine Coast Series
Waiting for Ana
The Trouble with Jack
Healing His Heart

Sunshine Coast Boxed Set

The Richards Brothers Series
The Trouble with Paradise
Marry in Haste
Outback Sunrise
Richards Brothers Boxed Set

Bondi Beach Love Series
Beach House
Beach Music
Beach Walk
Beach Dreams
The House on the Hill Boxed Set

Second Chance Bay Series
Her Outback Playboy
Her Outback Protector
Her Outback Haven
Her Outback Paradise
Boxed Set
The McDougalls of Second Chance Bay Set

Love Across Time Series
Come Back to Me
Follow Me
Finding Home
The Threads that Bind

Boxed Set
Love Across Time 1-4

Bindarra Creek Books
Worth the Wait
Full Circle
Secrets of River Cottage
A Clever Christmas
A Place to Belong
Hearts in Harmony

Awards

2025: Finalist- Romantic Suspense category - RUBY award-*From Across the Sea*

2023: Winner - Long contemporary novel category, RUBY award -*Larapinta.*

2023: Finalist - Australian Romance Readers Awards- *Kakadu Dawn,* the sixth and final book in the Porter Sisters series.

2018 and 2020: Finalist - for the NZ KORU Award.

2017: Winner - Best Established Author of the Year 2017 AUSROM

2017: Winner - Author of the Year, 2014 AUSROM
 Best Established Author, AUSROM Readers' Choice.

2016, 2017, 2018, 2019: Longlisted - Sisters in Crime Davitt Awards

2016: Finalist - Book of the Year, Long Romance, RWA Ruby Awards for *Kakadu Sunset*

2015: Winner - Best Established Author of the Year AUSROM

About the Author

Annie Seaton lives near the beach on the mid-north coast of New South Wales. Her career and studies spanned the education sector, including working as an academic research librarian, a high-school principal and a university tutor until she took early retirement and fulfilled her lifelong dream of a full-time writing career.

Each winter, Annie and her husband leave the beach to roam the remote areas of Australia for story ideas and research. She is passionate about preserving the beauty of the Australian landscape and respecting the traditional ownership of the land. For those readers who cannot experience this journey personally, Annie seeks to portray the natural beauty of the Australian environment—its spiritual locations, stunning landscapes and unique wildlife.

Readers can contact Annie through her website, annieseaton.net, or find her on

Facebook and Instagram.

www.ingramcontent.com/pod-product-compliance
Lightning Source LLC
Chambersburg PA
CBHW051701180726

48283CB00004B/1167